# SPARK

Happy reading! :)

Alex Zhang

EMBER

# ALEX ZHANG

# SPARK

BOOK ONE

Spark
© 2019 Alex Zhang

Published by LongTale Publishing

ISBN 978-1-941515-98-3

Library of Congress Control Number: 2019937420

Book design by Tamara Dever for TLC Graphics
www.TLCGraphics.com

Preliminary Editing by Eric Morris-Pusey
In-house Editor: Sharon Wilkerson


Photo of Alex by Alvin Gee Photography, Inc

# Contents

## CHAPTER 1

# Jackson Contemplates Strangling a TV Set

The sky was dark and overcast. Fat, swollen clouds lurked overhead as though waiting for the perfect moment to ruin Jackson's day. He absentmindedly ambled along a gray concrete sidewalk, hunching his shoulders against the cold as his breath fogged in the winter air.

The holiday had brought with it the looming threat of finals, which lurked in the dark recesses of Jackson's mind like an unwelcome guest at a party. He had looked over the thick mountain of reviews and study guides, then spent ten minutes coming up with an excuse to not do them, resolving to do absolutely nothing proactive for the next 24 hours.

Jackson stopped on the road to adjust his overlarge Christmas sweater, which had become awkwardly wedged on one of his shoulders. He had worried about putting the sweater on. It prominently featured Santa's bearded countenance on the front and was knitted from a type of wool just thick enough to be both uncomfortably itchy and uncomfortably warm. In the end, he'd decided to wear it than freeze to death. He was regretting his decision.

Jackson arrived at his bus stop, which consisted of a

worn wooden bench unceremoniously wedged at the edge of a sidewalk. It was comfortably situated above a sewer that was disgustingly pungent on a good day, while a gas mask would be useful on a bad one. Coincidentally, it was his favorite place to hang out on the weekends, maybe because it reminded him a little bit of himself.

Jackson pinched his nose shut as he plopped down onto the bench with a THUMP.

Another figure sat down beside Jackson, and he let out an inward sigh at the prospect of social interaction. He steeled his nerves and attempted to look as though he would punch the next person who attempted to talk to him.

The figure next to him snickered. "You look awfully stupid, Jack," the figure said. "More than usual, I mean."

Jack exhaled through his nose and laughed. "Dang, Wesley," he said. "I thought you were a stranger."

Wesley, a tall, thin boy with a head of black hair and dull green eyes, grinned at Jack. "You of all people should know by now that nobody comes through here."

"What's that supposed to mean?" Jack asked.

"Well, besides your obvious lack of people to interact with, you come here every day, don't you?" Wesley asked. "At least you've been here every time I've come."

"Where else am I supposed to go? I need a bus, don't I?"

Wesley sighed. "Dude, it's Saturday. This is a whole new level of pathetic. Don't you have anything to do?"

"Not really," Jack muttered glumly.

Wesley shrugged. "I'd criticize you for not studying for

finals, but even I can't muster the motivation."

"Why'd you come?" Jack asked.

"The family's out of town for the week, and you weren't over at your house," Wesley said, absentmindedly fiddling with his shirt buttons as he spoke. "You're very predictable, you know."

Before Jack could respond, a particularly fat raindrop delivered a sucker punch to Jack's forehead, causing him to flinch and look up. At some point during their conversation, it had begun to rain, light droplets of water falling from the sky and splattering onto the pavement.

Wesley followed Jack's gaze and pulled out an umbrella from inside his yellow raincoat. "Don't you ever read the weather forecast, Jack?" he asked with exasperation.

"Why would I do that when you already do it for me?" Jack retorted, standing up. Raindrops pattered on Wesley's umbrella, forming rivulets as they sloshed over the sides.

The two walked home in relative silence, their shoes squelching, already beginning to feel unpleasantly moist. Wesley whistled a tune of a song Jack couldn't quite identify. He spun his umbrella around, spraying rain every which way. The rain had steadily begun to form puddles, becoming more persistent as it continued to fall. Cars occasionally drove by. Typically, the only cars that Jack ever saw in his neighborhood were unwieldy and rusted, with broken windows covered with plastic wrap and loose trunk doors that bounced up and down as they moved. The monotony was occasionally broken with bullet holes, although they were becoming less of a rarity the harder Jack looked.

The freezing rain had practically swallowed the neighborhood by the time the boys arrived at Jack's house, both soaked and chilled to the bone.

"Should we knock?" Wesley asked, peering in through the grimy, unkempt glass of the front door.

"Dude, it's my house," Jack muttered, fumbling in his pockets for his house keys. "Why would we knock? Besides, it's not like anyone's home."

Jack drew out his house keys, their scuffed copper surfaces glinting dully in the dim light of the storm.

"I forgot how bad those looked," Wesley said, peering over Jack's shoulder. "You should get some new keys."

"What a waste of money. I'll get new ones when these stop working," Jack said, fiddling with the lock before the key finally turned with a satisfying click. The door swung open, revealing the den. A battered light brown couch squatted opposite a brick fireplace on the once white fur carpeting now tattered and grayish. Pictures of Jack were prominently placed upon the mantelpiece. Most of them were taken when he was young, and they all featured him in the most unflattering poses that were humanly possible. One photo showed his entire family looking at the camera. Jack, however had been caught mid-sneeze.

Wesley headed to the kitchen as Jack took off his sneakers and tossed them near the door, stripping off his sweater. He briefly contemplated punching the knitted Santa in the face before sighing and flinging it onto the couch. He slowly slid down onto the carpet as the storm raged outside. He grabbed a remote from between the cushions and switched on the box-like television which sat nearby. It was not quite old enough to have an antenna but not new enough to be flat or wall-mounted, either.

Wesley emerged from the kitchen holding a toaster, which he plugged into a nearby wall before taking out two packages of individually wrapped toaster strudels.

"What are we watching?" Wesley asked, putting the strudels into the toaster.

"The news, if I can get this thing to play," Jack said.

Wesley shrugged. "A bit boring, but at least I get to eat strudels."

"Who said that you could eat my strudels?" Jack asked.

Wesley raised a brow. "Strudels are temporary," he said, grandly gesturing. "Our friendship is forever."

Jack laughed. "Wow, that was pathetic," he said. "Eat the strudels if you want, but I'm fairly sure they're expired."

Wesley sighed and plopped onto the couch. "Is the TV not working?"

Jack frowned in consternation and rose up from the carpet. He fought the desire to pound on the television's top, looking for a way to solve the problem that didn't require anything beyond the base level knowledge of how a television worked. The TV screen buzzed with static, the crackling hisses and pops almost drowning out the storm outside.

Jack was about to resort to fiddling with the dials when

a bolt of lightning flashed outside.

Jack wasn't afraid of lightning, but this bolt was a big one- a thick column of pure energy which shattered the gray sky as it arced down to earth. Although he prepared himself for the inevitable noise, he was still almost knocked off his feet when a clap of thunder rang through the house as loud and intensely as though someone had fired a cannon. The television rattled and wobbled. The screen flickered and shook before going out entirely.

Jack looked around the room before he had realized the television screen had taken on an almost water-like quality to it. The television glass rippled and ebbed as a dark and indistinct shape appeared behind its surface. The shape moved to and fro for a second, dawdling just behind the television's glassy surface before suddenly surging outwards. As it cleared the glass, Jack saw that it was a gloved hand. The hand groped its way around for a second before it found the edge of the television. An arm emerged, clad in a tuxedo.

"Hey, what's happening?" Jack asked.

"Well, it seems pretty obvious to me," Wesley said. "Somebody's climbing out of your TV."

"Doesn't that…weird you out a little bit?" Jack asked.

"Not particularly. We should probably make room for whoever's coming through," Wesley suggested.

"That would be nice," a voice said.

Jack watched as the top half of a man emerged from the television. The man seemed to be having difficulty extracting his bottom half.

"This is quite undignified," the man said. "I must say, I thought your television would be bigger, Jackson."

Jack sighed. "Since this doesn't usually happen to me, and you know my name, I'm going to assume that you're supernatural."

The man beamed at Jack. He had a mouthful of oddly sharp teeth, as though he'd filed them down to points. His eyes were strangely iridescent, shifting from purple to green to blue as he swiveled his head about the room. "Excellent! I was wondering how I would explain this to you, but you seem rather cool with my being here."

Jack gave the man a look of baffled amusement. "Do you need help getting out of the TV?" he asked.

Wesley snickered.

The man sighed. "No, I'm fine," he said.

"You're clearly not fine," Jack said, gesturing at the man's predicament.

"Well, I'm not, but I think I can solve this on my own," the man said, putting a hand on either side of him on the television. There was an audible hissing sound, as though something rather large had been dunked into a vat of boiling water. The gloves glowed bright orange for a brief moment before the television crumbled into dust.

The rest of the man emerged from the remnants of the TV, brushing the dust off of his black dress pants as he did so. Jack stared at the gray dust pile on the carpet, his mouth agape.

"Well, that was uncalled for," Wesley said through a mouthful of toaster strudel.

"Yes, that was," the man agreed. "My deepest apologies." The man snapped his fingers, and the dust swirled around in a miniature tornado, forming an indistinct outline of a television. The cloud parted, revealing a deformed television in a shade of lime green so hideously garish that Jack briefly wondered if the man was color blind.

"See? All fixed," the man said, grinning again.

"Wow, I can't tell the difference," Jack said. "It's almost like it never disappeared at all."

"My name's Subulo. Jack, Wesley, we're going on an adventure. No need to thank me," he proclaimed.

There was a brief moment of awkward silence following his announcement.

"Uh, no we're not," Wesley said. "Sounds fun, but we were taught not to go on *adventures* with strangers, particularly ones who come out of a TV."

Subulo sighed. "Look, Wesley," he said. "I'm gonna level with you. This house...this is Jack's house, right? This house looks very nice, right?"

Wesley gave him a bemused look. "It's nice, I guess?"

Subulo nodded. "Well, it's going to be destroyed in about..." he checked his watch. "In about five minutes. Four minutes and thirty seconds, to be precise."

"Is that a threat?" Wesley asked. "I can't exactly do anything about it if it is, I just want clarification."

Subulo shook his head. "No. I ran into a wee bit of trouble and just managed to escape my pursuers. I thought I'd kill two birds with one stone, though, because I still have a company quota to meet and your house was the only populated one that was nearby. Any other questions?"

Jack cleared his throat. "Do we have any say in the matter?"

"No, not really," the man said. "We really have to go."

Subulo winced as another ear-splitting thunderclap shook the room.

"Time to do the thing," he muttered to himself. "Jackson, you wouldn't happen to have any chalk on you, would you?"

"No, I don't," Jack said. "Get out of my house."

"Aren't you listening, Jackson?" Subulo said, waltzing into the kitchen and rummaging through the cabinets. "There won't be a house for very long." He removed a pen from one of the drawers. "I suppose a pen will do."

"What are you going to do with that pen?" Jack asked. Subulo was holding an antique pen that Jack's father had given him.

"Well, I'm going to use the pen to graffiti your walls with pagan symbols," Subulo said. "And then we're getting the heck out of dodge."

Jack stood up. "Look, I want to say that it's been nice to meet you, but it hasn't. Can you take your problems elsewhere?"

Subulo looked back at Jack. His eyes flashed a shade of crimson as he uncapped the pen.

"Look, Jack," Subulo said. "I'd love to take my problems elsewhere, but I'm all out of juice. I can't climb through any more televisions for at least a couple of hours."

Jack gave a resigned sigh and slumped back onto the couch, burying his face in his hands. "I just wanted to watch the news, man," he said to Wesley.

"Pretty disappointing for a first encounter with the supernatural," Wesley said. "At least he hasn't asked for money."

Subulo cackled as he defaced Jack's living room walls, the pen making sharp scratching sounds as it scraped against the plaster. The room's temperature sharply rose, and then plunged downwards, dropping so quickly that Jack swore he could feel the water on his clothes beginning to freeze.

Jack peered behind him. Subulo had managed to deface an astonishing amount of Jack's property in a matter of minutes, scratching out all manner of heathenish images upon the walls. The ink was so smudged and jumbled that the images had begun to blend together. Jack could see the faint outlines of pentagrams, various letters and words written in a slanting foreign script, and several smiley faces arranged seemingly at random along the walls.

"What are you doing?" Jack moaned in despair.

"Nothing that you need to worry about," Subulo said, capping the pen and tossing it to Jack. The point had been worn to a rounded dull metal nub, the exquisitely handcrafted wooden barrel smudged with ink and sweat.

"Are you done destroying my property?" Jack asked. "Can you leave now?"

"There was never a me, and there never was a you," Subulo grinned. "There was only us. And yes, we are going."

Jack opened his mouth to retort, but was drowned out by another thunderclap.

"Man, how the heck is the thunder so loud?" Wesley muttered.

Subulo chuckled. "That wasn't thunder."

Jack frowned. "What do you..."

*BOOM.*

Now that Jack listened, he could see what Subulo meant. Although the noise sounded with the same earth-shattering, ear-splitting force, it wasn't thunder. It was something more...solid.

The sound was becoming more frequent. *BOOM. BOOM.*

Wesley had gone very pale.

Subulo grinned. "If that's what I think it is, it's very large, very strong, and very eager to kill us."

"Very eager to kill *you*, you mean," Jack muttered. "We're just collateral damage."

Subulo shrugged. "I won't deny it," he said. "Are you ready to go now?"

They both nodded. *BOOM. BOOM. BOOM.*

Subulo rubbed his gloved hands together. "That's what I like to see!" he exclaimed. "Alright, everybody! Through the television!"

The two boys turned in unison and looked incredulously at Subulo.

"I hope you're not being serious," Wesley said.

"I'm not, geez," Subulo said. "There's a minivan parked behind the house."

## CHAPTER 2

# Bullets Don't Get Along Terribly Well With Canines

"A minivan...I don't have time," Jack muttered. "Let's just go before I change my mind."

"How are you planning to escape with a minivan?" Wesley asked. "They aren't exactly famed for being fast."

Subulo said, "Every minute we stand here is a minute wasted, my friend. If we don't hit the road soon, I might just go by myself."

"Subulo, that thing sounds like it's eating my house," Jack said, peeking through the window. "What the...there's a hole the size of east Texas in my yard, dude. How do you plan to stop this from ravaging the neighborhood?"

Subulo shook his head. "We...and by we, I mean supernatural beings...don't typically affect the *normal* world. How do I put this? It's like we exist on a different layer of reality, only slightly tethered to yours. Luckily for you, I've brought you into my reality with me, so now you can be killed by whatever is chasing us."

"How is that lucky?" Jack grumbled.

"Well, you can experience what the world has to offer," he said. Subulo scratched his chin as he opened the back door.

"What a lame excuse," Jack said. "I don't suppose that my house could've been spared?"

"Nope," Subulo said cheerfully. "It was doomed the moment you laid eyes on me."

The boys followed Subulo out of the back door. The rain had intensified. The dark sky glowered at them from above, soot-black thunderclouds gathering like thick wisps of smoke. A beetle-red minivan sat in the driveway, the driver's side door slightly ajar.

Subulo hustled the boys into the backseat, sprinting around the side and practically hurling himself through the driver's side door. He pulled out a pair of car keys and turned them in the ignition. The car roared to life as Jack shifted in the backseat.

"Subulo, why are there claw marks on the seats?" Jack asked.

"Yeah," Wesley added, "and what's with the bullet holes?"

"Re-upholstery is expensive," Subulo dismissively said from the front seat. "I'm not going to pay for it until the seats are covered in blood, and even then I still might not."

Jack nodded. "Fair enough."

The minivan made ominous coughing noises as it pulled out of the driveway, the windshield wipers agitatedly swishing back and forth as rain pounded the car. The group sat in silence for a moment as the car noisily sped down the road.

"So," Subulo said, resolutely facing forward. "I forgot to mention that I'll be picking someone else up along the way."

"Someone else?" Wesley asked nervously. "Are they…"

"She's not supernatural, unless you count her uncannily bad temper," Subulo said. "You don't really need to worry about her for now."

"Subulo?" Jack asked from the backseat. "Out of curiosity, when is my life going to return to normal?"

Subulo groaned. "I wish you'd stop with the dumb questions, Jack," he said. "I've taken what you call a 'normal life' and beaten it to death with a club. It's best that you don't look at the corpse, as it'll only make you yearn for a time that's long gone at this point. Same goes for you, Wesley."

Jack was quiet for a moment, and then rubbed his temples in dismay.

"Alright," he said. "So, you've essentially destroyed my life in the space of a few minutes."

"Isn't that what I just said?" Subulo asked from the front seat.

Jack felt a dread that he hadn't felt in quite a long time begin to claw at his well-maintained composure, threatening to push him over the edge. He took several deep breaths.

"What will become of my parents?" Jack asked.

"My superiors will probably arrange something for them," Subulo said. "You and Wesley will either be classified as missing persons or will be presumed dead."

Jack leaned back in the seat.

Wesley spoke, his voice oddly hoarse. "The rain's stopped," he said.

The windshield wipers lay still and unmoving upon the dash. The only sounds now were occasional splashes as the minivan plowed through puddles.

"Weren't we being chased by something?" Wesley continued. "A rather noisy something, in fact?"

Subulo checked his watch. "Right on point, Wesley," he said. "It's rather concerning that we're no longer hearing it. In fact, I should probably…"

CRUNCH.

The minivan buckled to the side as a large something tore a chunk out of the back of it, letting in a gust of cold air.

"Well, that was unexpected," Subulo said. "Looks like my pursuers are more interested than I thought."

His foot lowered, and the minivan unsteadily lurched forward, leaning dangerously close to the tipping point as the something attempted to take another bite out of it. Snapping noises could be heard from the back, as well as canine-esque snarling noises reminiscent of a bloodhound hawking phlegm. The car inched forward as Jack nervously stared at the opening at the back of it.

"Not to worry you, but I can see that thing's teeth," Jack called to the front.

"I'm not worried in the slightest," Subulo said, pulling out a handgun from the front cup-holder and tossing it to Jack. "Shoot it, will you? I can't aim and drive at the same time."

Jack's hands trembled as he clutched the handgun, a

rather oddly shaped gun with an overlarge barrel similar to a revolver's. It was made entirely out of an oddly sleek and shiny material, which glinted black in the overhead lights. There was no discernible trigger, nor was there any place to insert ammunition.

"How exactly am I supposed to fire this?" Jack asked.

"Point it at what you're trying to shoot and tell it to," Subulo said from the front.

Jack blinked in confusion. "Like, 'shoot this, gun?'"

"Well, it has a name, but yeah," Subulo said, as though it was the most obvious thing in the world. "Have you used guns before, Jack?"

"I haven't, but I'm about ninety-percent sure that they're not voice-activated yet," Jack said.

CRUNCH. The van screeched in agony as a large section of the back peeled away, exposing what exactly was gnawing at it.

Jack took one look at what he was supposed to be shooting at, and what little resolve he'd had to begin with withered away in one fell swoop.

"I'm supposed to be shooting that?" he incredulously asked. "Where do I even aim for?"

"I'm with you on this," Wesley said. "Is everything in the supernatural realm this ugly?"

A huge, vaguely canine hunk of flesh had sunk its teeth into the floor of the van, its paws scrabbling at Jack and Wesley. It had a snout and two front paws, and the resemblance to a dog ended about there. It was covered in black scales, with patches of scraggly crimson fur poking through the gaps. It regarded the boys with beady orange eyes, placed on either side of its face. The midsection of its torso seemed to congeal into a thick, viscous black slime, which floated along behind the abomination, swaying to and fro as the car moved forward. It was as though a menagerie of animals had mated with the resulting product having a bottom half chopped cleanly off and replaced with several tubs of rancid Jell-o.

"I'll pretend I didn't hear that, Wesley," Subulo said, glancing backwards. "I think that's a hell-hound."

"That's a hell-hound?" Jack asked. "Isn't it supposed to be more hound and less… gelatin?"

"Well, a hell-hound is formally defined as any supernatural creature that can trace its origins back to canine roots, with the exception of the more well-known ones," Subulo said. "It just helps lexicographers deal with the headaches of having to classify every grotesque result of forced breeding that lives to see the light of day. I'm pretty sure this is one of those results. Here, let me try something."

Subulo pulled the car into a sharp turn around a street corner, slamming the hell-hound into a stop sign. The hound's teeth remained resolutely buried into the floor. The hound tried to drag itself further into the car with its paws, growling. The only thing that seemed to be stopping it was the fact that it couldn't seem to remove its teeth from the carpet. It made frustrated snarling noises as it futilely clawed at the boys, its eyes fixed on the gun.

"Does he have to shoot it?" Wesley asked. "It seems to be fine for now."

As soon as the words had left his lips, the hound freed itself from the floor, yanking its teeth out as the van shrieked in protest. It barked at them, seemingly still wary of the firearm in Jack's hand.

"You were saying?" Subulo asked. "This couldn't be simpler. Just tell the gun to fire."

The hell-hound was beginning to grow bold. It experimentally snapped at Jack, its jaws thick with reddish slime.

Jack hesitantly pointed the gun at the hell-hound. It tensed, crouching down and getting ready to lunge.

"Gun, sic 'em!" Subulo cried, just as the hell-hound pounced.

The gun writhed in Jack's hand. The overlong barrel ballooned outwards, expanding into a tentacle like appendage which wrapped around the hell-hound. The tip grew sharp and pointy as it pressed against the hell-hound's temple, forming into a spike before it disappeared into the hell-hound's head. The thing began to shriek helplessly as the gun burrowed its way through, beginning to protrude on the other side of its head. Jack felt a pang of sympathy for the hell-hound as its head was turned into several slices of impromptu kebab. Soon, the thing's screams subsided, the gun's barrel shrinking back to its usual size as the hell-hound's inert corpse hit the floor with a wet thwack, dark reddish blood pooling on the carpeted floor.

"Neat, isn't it?" Subulo asked from the front seat. "The gun, not the hell-hound."

"I don't think that that's a gun," Wesley said. "It's shaped like a gun, sure, but guns tend to fire bullets and such."

Although Jack couldn't see Subulo, he could imagine him rolling his eyes. "Whatever, dude," he said. "Kick the corpse out of the van."

"Wouldn't that worry the pedestrians?" Wesley asked.

"Considering that they can't see the corpse, not really," Subulo said. "I'm just trying to throw off anyone that might be following us, because this thing's leaking blood like a burst ketchup packet."

Jack experimentally prodded the corpse with his shoe. The blood was proving to be curiously sticky and warm against his feet, clinging to his shoe as he drew it back. "Why is the blood so sticky?" he asked to no one in particular.

"Your guess is as good as mine," Subulo said. "Ditch the corpse. Quickly."

Jack sighed as he knelt on the van's floor next to the corpse. The hell-hound had begun to reek, the flesh rotting at a curiously fast pace as Jack rolled the corpse out of the van, smearing various bits of bloodied flesh and brain matter across the upholstery. The hell-hound hit the road with a *THWACK*.

"It's gone now, right?" Subulo asked.

"Yes," Jack said.

"Just out of curiosity, what happened to the other pursuer?" Wesley asked. "The one that was presumably larger than the hell-hound."

Subulo shrugged. "It's probably lost us by now," he said. "Jack, you'll be happy to know that your house has been spared. If I have time, I'll swing by to scrub the ink off later."

"Does that mean I can go home?" Jack asked.

"No," Subulo said. "If you could see the hell-hound, it means that my pursuers think that you're aiding me. You're now just as much of a target as I am."

Behind them, Jack heard the unmistakable rumbling sound of an explosion. He turned around and saw reddish flames licking at the sky, great plumes of smoke rising in the distance.

"Did the hell-hound just...explode?" Jack asked.

"Yup," Subulo said. "Jackson, Wesley, put on your seat-belts."

The boys complied, strapping themselves in. "Why do we need to put on our seat-belts?" Wesley asked curiously.

"So many questions," Subulo said. "You'll find out in a minute."

He pressed down on the pedal, and the car sped forward at a pace unrivaled by anything previously. The passing scenery of shabby, derelict houses turned into a grayish-brown blur as the minivan picked up speed. As Jack peered out through the windshield, he realized that Subulo was headed straight for a large evergreen tree that was growing in a nearby yard.

"Hey, Subulo," he said, panic creeping into his voice.

Subulo didn't respond. The car continued speeding

towards the tree. The tree appearing larger and closer through the windshield.

"Subulo," Jack said again. "I quite like being alive, so why don't we..."

Just before the car collided with the evergreen, it pitched downwards through the ground. As the car plunged downwards, its fall began to slow. The air took on a curious, molasses-like quality. It became harder and harder to breathe as they continued to descend. A curious scent of lavender filled the air, accompanied by a purple light, which enveloped the car in a soft purple glow. The car was falling so slowly that it felt like they were moving in slow-motion.

"Where exactly are we?" Wesley inquired, glancing all around him. "Why is there purple light everywhere?"

"Well, we've either spontaneously died or I've transported us to where we need to be," Subulo said. "We're going to stage a heist on an elevator. *Or of an elevator.*"

"What use do we have for an elevator?" Jack asked, rolling down the window and peering out of it. "Also, are we in the middle of nowhere?"

"Well, the elevator is going to have someone in it who I require the use of," Subulo said. "And no, we're not in the middle of nowhere. We're in Hendeku, which is about the closest you'll ever get to a proper Hell. There's not fire and brimstone and such, and eternal torture was given up in favor of just having the damned kill each other."

"What exactly does this have to do with an elevator?" Wesley asked. "Why is there an elevator down here?"

"Well, the damned can buy their way out of Hendeku by killing enough people, which is kind of a dumb rule," Subulo said. "But our friend is about to come through here."

"Does that mean that your friend has killed a lot of people?" Jack nervously asked. "I don't particularly want to be acquainted with a murderer."

"Jack, if you're going to survive, we're going to have to get your moral compass surgically removed at some point," Subulo said. "And her name is Ruby. No, she hasn't killed a lot of people, despite what I previously said. On a related note, straighten your hair, both of you. I think I hear elevator music."

Jack strained his ears. In fact, he could hear the heady tones of Muzak wafting steadily from below.

"Open the car doors," Subulo said. "We're going to have to liberate the elevator."

Jack complied, opening the doors.

"Jump out of the car," Subulo called to him.

"I'm not a big fan of untimely death," Jack called back.

"If the air's thick enough to support a car, it can support you, Jackson," Subulo said. "Look, see? I've climbed out already."

Jack looked. Sure enough, Subulo was suspended in midair, slowly drifting upwards as though he was in outer space.

Jackson took a deep breath of the curiously thick air before leaping out of the car. His stomach dropped for a moment as he contemplated falling to his death, but the air supported him. He had the curious sensation of being in a swimming pool full of gelatin. Wesley followed Jack.

The Muzak got louder. A distant light appeared below them.

"How exactly are you planning to 'liberate' the elevator?" Wesley asked.

"It's simple," Subulo said. "I've loaded the minivan full of leaden weights. As soon as the elevator becomes susceptible to gravity, I'll throw it on top of it."

"Simple, huh," Wesley said, his face pale. "I guess I'll leave you to it, then."

The elevator was getting closer. It had reached the point where they could actually see what appeared to be a stereotypical elevator, composed of stainless steel and marble. As the elevator approached, Subulo hefted the car as though it weighed nothing, then casually lobbed it upwards. The minivan sailed upwards for a moment, imperceptibly stopping for a fraction of a second before it began to fall downwards once more, connecting with the top of the elevator. There was an almighty *CRASH* as the elevator ground to a halt.

"Just to clarify, she isn't a murderer, right?" Jack asked, hesitantly backing away from the elevator.

"No," Subulo said, drifting down next to Jack. "Why are you so oddly fixated on the subject?"

"I guess I just like keeping my organs intact," Jack said. "Not all of us have the suicidal courage needed to try to out-drive a hell-hound."

"I could've out driven the hell-hound, given enough time," Subulo grumbled. "But never mind that."

"Aren't the doors supposed to be opening?" Wesley asked, giving the elevator a nervous look.

"No," Subulo said. "I'm putting the elevator on the van."

## CHAPTER 3

# Ruby Patiently Waits for an Old Man to Remember His Own Name

Ruby Jones scampered to the top of a large, stout boulder, casting her gaze around the meadow. A river flowed past, ghost-like white fish flapping their fins as they darted about in the murky, amethyst-colored water. Gnarled wisteria trees stretched twisted branches across the lavender-colored sky, enveloping the riverbanks with low-hanging violet flowers, their scent almost repulsive in its intensity.

She looked down at her kid sister, Amber, who was washing her clothes in the river. The water had an airy quality to it; the clothes instantly drying upon leaving the water, the droplets rushing down the worn cotton to rejoin the river. A menagerie of black-feathered birds roosted in the wisteria trees, preening themselves and occasionally croaking to one another in voices that sounded human. She had noticed early on that most of the birds lacked eyes, and the ones that had eyes were invariably blind.

Her mother had kept birds; two parakeets, one green, one red. Both had vanished without explanation. Initially, they had suspected the cat, but then it had disappeared as well. If Ruby strained her memory hard enough, she could remember their names, worn relics of the past, long since gone.

Ruby breathed in the scent of violets. Amber finished the laundry, methodically folding their garments and loading them into a stained canvas rucksack.

Ruby effortlessly slid down the boulder, leaving several scraps of her pants along the way to sharp crevices in the rock. "I'm bored," she announced, scooping up Amber. "Let's go somewhere."

Amber, who was approaching the tender age of ten, dispassionately glanced at Ruby. "A funny thing happened today, Ruby," she said. "I forgot my own name when I woke."

Ruby let out a sigh. Amber was always like this; her sister was surprisingly pessimistic and morbid for someone her age, undoubtedly a side effect of being raised in such a ghoulish environment. Ruby had only managed to keep herself sane and functioning through her own relentless optimism, but Amber rode the wave of dread and fear like a professional surf boarder.

Ruby forced a smile. "That sounds like something we can talk about on the way to the Booth."

The Booth was a black telephone booth, located in the middle of a ruined strip mall near the wisteria grove. Besides being a spot designated as neutral ground, it also was where the damned could shell out funds to become reborn.

Amber sighed. "Do what you want," she said. "It's just a waste of time, though. It's not like we have enough."

They walked away from the grove, Amber with both

hands in the pockets of an old yellow raincoat and the rucksack slung over her shoulder.

They walked out of the shade of the wisteria trees into an abandoned road. The pavement had been shifted aside as wild tangles of weeds grew in massive cracks in the sidewalk. The road was littered with craters and sinkholes, in some places even peeling away into the sewer systems below, releasing a foul stench into the air that made Ruby nostalgic for the scent of the violets.

Ruby could barely make out the husks of bombed-out buildings in the distance as they walked down the road, the vast, ruined concrete fingers grasping at the sky providing testament to how hard the fall of man had been. To their left, scraggly weeds and vines had made themselves at home in the pavement, huge labyrinthine columns of yellow and green snaking up and down the sidewalk and tunneling up nearby walls. The strip mall containing the Booth was situated on their right, glass fragments littering the ground in front of it. It had a name once, but the letters had been worn away as time went on. Ruby strode up to the front of the mall and pushed the glass door open. They entered the mall and walked past rows and rows of ruined shops until they finally arrived at the atrium. Light filtered in through the grimy glass roof, the rays catching motes of floating dust as it shone on the Booth. It was less a booth than a box, composed entirely of brass that had been darkened with soot and ash. Ruby strode up to the door of the Booth and knocked on it, smudging her knuckles in the process.

A man in a purple pork pie hat and silver spectacles opened the door, peering at Amber and Ruby with kindly dark eyes.

"Hello, old man," said Ruby.

"Oh, it's you," said the old man, visibly unexcited.

"Might I add how dashing your hat looks. It really goes well with your…well-groomed age lines," Ruby said with an innocent tone.

The old man stared at Ruby before erupting into laughter. "That was a good one," he roared. "But I can't let people across for free, you know. It's not worth my job."

"Why even charge a price?" Amber broke in.

The old man sighed. "Sorry, Amber. The higher-ups demand it of us toll workers. If I had it my way, only the repentant would be able to cross back over. This monetary system is quite overrated."

"Can I leave a divine IOU or something like that?" Ruby asked.

The old man cracked a smile. "Sorry, Ruby," he said. "No can do."

"Are you sure?" Ruby asked.

The old man paused a moment. "I don't know if I should, but…"

*BANG.* A bullet struck the tiled floor of the mall.

"That's my cue to leave," said the old man, ducking back into the Booth.

"Oh, great," said Ruby sarcastically. "Could you leave us alone for a moment? I was in the middle of something."

There wasn't a response. A second bullet struck the tiled floor.

No time for chatting, she thought, taking Amber's hand. "Remember what I told you, right?"

"Essential survival tactics," Amber said solemnly. "Shoot the ones who're shooting at us. Very useful, by the way."

Ruby kneaded her forehead with her hands. "Hide behind the Booth for now," she said, pulling out a pistol that she'd nicked from a corpse a couple of weeks prior.

Amber complied, shifting into a crouch.

Bullets ricocheted off of the tiled floors, pinging around the room whilst Ruby casually loaded her pistol, pulling back the slide with a click. She took a moment to marvel at how horrendous her opponent's aim was before she sprinted towards a nearby elevator. The doors had been pried open long ago, the steel cables cut. Ruby looked down and cursed as she realized the strip mall had a basement level.

Although she wasn't used to climbing up elevator shafts, she assumed it wouldn't be too different from climbing any other kind of rope. She grabbed hold of a steel cable and experimentally yanked it downwards. Upon discovering that it held fast, she shimmied onto it, hesitantly putting more and more weight on the cable before she threw herself onto it. The cable swayed dangerously as she shimmied upwards towards the next set of elevator doors, panic beginning to set in as she surveyed the drop below her.

Ruby cursed again as she felt her palms moisten. Why was she forced to burden this crippling fear of heights?

Her grip became viselike on the cable as she slowly moved upwards.

*If I get ambushed up here, I will piss myself, scream, and then fall to an embarrassing death,* she grimly thought to herself as her arms began to shake.

Slowly, agonizingly, she made her way up to the second floor.

The elevator doors were firmly shut.

Ruby very nearly slipped off the cables as panic began to consume her. Her flight or fight response was in full force, which only made matters worse as she couldn't do either. As luck would have it, the elevator shaft was just thin enough that Ruby could brace her weight against one side and put her legs on the other, which made her wonder how small the elevator had been.

She held in that position, instantly regretting her decision when her back began to hurt. It was reminiscent of an invisible chair position, only with the added consequence of death. With very little time to spare, Ruby decided the best course of action was to shoot the door. In one fluid motion, she affixed a silencer to her pistol, aimed it, and let loose a clip of twelve bullets directly into the door. With any luck, not only had she forced it open, but she'd also killed anything that was lurking in front of it lying in wait to ambush her. She heaved her way upwards until she was in position to kick the doors open. The odds were 50/50 that her feet would bounce off the doors and lead to her demise.

As the doors snapped open, Ruby tucked her legs in and

rolled into action, a move that left her completely exposed to enemy fire for several seconds as she struggled to recover from the clumsy somersault.

After assessing her surroundings, she realized that not only was there a staircase, but that it had also been directly next to the elevator.

"Son-of-a..."

"Don't move." A deep voice with at hint of an English accent spoke from directly behind her. Ruby felt what she thought was the barrel of a gun pressed against her head.

Ruby, being smart enough to get herself into the situation to begin with, calmly began to turn around.

"Freeze," the voice said. "Don't trifle with me, woman."

Ruby froze. "You might possibly be the least stupid person I've met down here," she murmured. "What are you planning on doing? I don't have anything of value on me."

The voice sighed. "Look, I've been ordered to kill you."

"Who would care enough to order you to kill me?" she asked, attempting to act nonchalant even though her hands had begun to tremble.

"It doesn't really matter at this point," the voice said. "I should really get on with this now. It was nice meeting you."

In a moment of pure desperation, Ruby lurched forward, throwing her pistol behind her. She felt a bullet graze the side of her cheek, wincing as she spun around to face her would-be killer.

"Good heavens, you're ugly," she murmured, pulling out a second pistol from a holster on her belt.

The thing that Ruby faced wasn't human; that was clear enough. Its face was a mass of writhing, gelatinous pink flesh. Three hard, mandible-like appendages protruded from its face, making the thing look like a half-melted pink marshmallow getting stabbed through by a fork. It was dressed in what could've passed for an ill-fitting Santa Claus outfit, with overly large crimson robes and a matching velvet hat. Now that she listened closely, she found that it didn't possess vocal chords, or at least she didn't think so; it seemed to communicate by vibrating its head to form a slightly warped approximation of human speech.

"I get that a lot," the thing pleasantly vibrated. "It's usually the last thing they say."

Ruby, seeing that she had the upper hand, seized on the opportunity by planting several bullets into its face. It shrieked in pain before dropping to the ground, oozing a yellowish pus onto the dusty white floor.

Ruby wiped sweat off her brow before bending down to retrieve her other pistol.

"That wasn't very nice."

Ruby looked up to see the thing rising, dripping pus onto its outfit as it did so. "Oh, yuck," she said. "Can you not, please?"

"You can't kill me, I'm afraid," the thing said, pulling out a revolver from the depths of its robes. "I'm effectively immortal. Eternal, you might say...OW!"

Ruby abruptly ended the conversation with a bullet. After the thing hit the ground again, she snatched the revolver before turning tail and sprinting away. She vaulted over the glass enclosure on the second floor and onto the tiled floor of the atrium. Amber was still crouched behind the Booth, looking decidedly bored.

"Amber, I'm gathering that you know how to aim a gun," Ruby said.

"I do, yes," Amber said. "Do I get to shoot something for once?"

Ruby nodded, wiping the gunk off of the revolver before tossing the gun to Amber. She felt the revolver for a moment, spinning the chamber before she nodded. "This will do," Amber pronounced.

Ruby heard a *THUD*.

"My legs," the thing listlessly groaned. It seemed to have hurled itself from the second floor before gaining full control of its body, and was now curled up in a puddle of its own blood, staining the floor. Ruby felt something close to pity as she looked at it.

"Yikes, dude," Ruby said. "You're surprisingly incompetent."

She aimed a pistol at the thing's head, but just as she was about to fire, it exploded, spraying stray entrails and greenish, putrid-smelling viscera every which way.

"I know I've said this before, but yuck," Ruby said, gagging a little. "What a disappointing conclusion."

She turned away. "Do you think that the old man will let us in now?" she asked.

Amber shrugged. "You'll be happy to know that you

35

won't have your answer yet," she said, pointing to where the thing's corpse had exploded. "It's moving again."

Ruby face-palmed. "I don't have time for this," she said, turning back around. "How is there enough left of you that you can still move?"

The thing's head seemed to have abandoned human speech entirely, settling for making random buzzing noises as it floated upwards. The red robes followed, being dragged upwards before they slumped once more to the ground. The head seemed to have detached itself from the body, becoming a floating, writhing ball of flesh. As Ruby watched, the ball began to speed towards her, trailing guts and stray pieces of pink tissue.

Ruby sighed and took aim. BANG. Although the bullet found its mark, it only seemed to further enrage the thing, which, if anything, began to go even faster. Ruby ducked as it sailed over her head, its momentum becoming too great for it to recover. It smacked into a nearby display case, getting a faceful of glass shards. Although it had been ineffective, she still felt obliged to shoot it once again.

"Ugh, forget this," it warbled. "I'll settle for one."

BANG.

Ruby whirled around to see Amber slump to the floor, an expression of mild surprise upon her face. The thing's body had stood up, the robes sloughing off of its shoulders as it tucked the revolver back into its robes.

"We'll meet some other time, Ruby," the head said, soaring out of the display case and attaching itself back onto its body. "For now, this is goodbye. Again, it was lovely to meet the both of you."

Ruby said nothing. She felt something hollow in the pit of her stomach. Her heart hurt for some reason.

Amber had long since died when Ruby approached.

Ruby didn't really know how to deal with this. She'd seen death before, but this was... different.

Maybe it was because she loved Amber, or maybe because she was so young. Maybe it was because she seemed so small and alone, lying on the white tile floor without having fired a single shot from her gun. Ruby didn't quite know how to react. She felt as though she'd been shoved on stage without any lines and then asked to perform. She felt out of place.

She stumbled over to Amber, and slumped to the ground. Amber's skin was deathly cold to touch. She couldn't bring herself to weep, it seemed.

So she sat.

She sat for quite a while. There weren't any sentimental memories of Amber. They'd mostly just existed, living from day to day upon the barren hellscape. She'd never imagine that it'd end this way, and yet here she was.

After what might've been years, the door to the Booth opened.

The old man peeked out from the door, his pork pie hat askew. His face brightened when he saw Ruby.

"Ah!" he cried. "It's Ruby! You're still...alive..." His gaze had drifted to the body which lay slumped nearby.

He fell silent.

"Well, things happen," he said at last. He took off his spectacles. In that moment, he seemed to visibly age as he let out a pained sigh. "I've seen too much to offer you an empty consolation. You don't deserve it, and it's beneath me to give one to you."

Ruby nodded. She understood, painful as it was to admit it to herself. She had attempted to prepare herself for a situation like this. The world they lived in was unforgiving and brutal, with death lurking around every corner, but her efforts were all for naught. Her relentless optimism had vanished, leaving her an emotionless husk.

"Well, I guess it's time for you to step into the Booth," the old man said. "It's as good a time as any, I suppose."

Ruby stepped into the Booth. It was cramped. A telephone was on the wall. The old man was surprisingly tall; his head scraped the Booth's ceiling when he stood upright.

"Hold on," the old man said. "I could've sworn that...ah, here we are."

He pulled a switch, and the Booth was plunged into darkness. "There we go."

The lights came back on. Ruby was no longer standing in a phone booth.

She was in what appeared to be an airport terminal. The ground was covered in striped carpet. Rows of black-leather and metal chairs were tightly packed together, arranged into neat, organized rows. Several free-standing suitcases were scattered throughout the terminal, in colors and patterns ranging from blank white to leopard print. Large floor-to-ceiling windows showcased a view overlooking a vast, purple-tinted nothingness.

"Nice view," she absentmindedly said.

"I know," said the old man. "You'd think they'd give me a view of a snowy mountaintop or something like that. Nope. Being an inter-realm regulator isn't that great. I used to be a deity, you know. And not a small one, either. I think my name was…Hermann? No, that's not right."

The man lapsed into silence.

"Ah. Yes. Hermie," he said. "No, wait. That's not right either." He clapped his hands together. "Hermes! I remember now. I was the god of traveling and thievery and all sorts of other stuff. I forget from which country I came from. They just call me *Bernard* here, though."

"What should I call you, then?" Ruby asked, not quite paying attention to the old man.

He man scratched his beard. "Just call me Bernard. I'm more likely to respond to that."

"Ok then, Bernard," Ruby said. "Why am I here, exactly?"

"I'm glad you asked that!" Bernard beamed. "You see, I'm here to save you from this place."

"Save me? From here?" Ruby asked. "Why would you do that?"

The man shrugged. "Well, you kept me company. You're a lot nicer than the average company that I keep. This place is for the damned, after all, and you'd beat criminals and murderers any day. I don't want to see you die as well. The least I can do is offer a chance at redemption."

"I can't pay," Ruby said.

"Don't worry about paying," Bernard said. "I'll take care of everything."

He walked up to a white desk near one of the windows. A computer was chirping and buzzing on it. He typed something onto it, and a white slip of paper churned out of the side, and he handed it to her.

"Keep this in your hand, otherwise you'll be forcefully dumped back here, probably in multiple pieces. It's a one-way ticket to the surface world." The old man smiled at her, his eyes twinkling.

"Thanks, Bernard," Ruby said.

"It's no problem," he declared. "Well, it is, but it's worth it. You brought me the happiest times I've had in many centuries. I'm sorry if I didn't show that I appreciated you much, but just know that I did."

He paused. "Well, it's time for your reincarnation. Remember, all your memories will disappear in an instant. And don't drop the ticket!"

He guided her to an elevator door. Ruby stepped into the elevator and turned to look at Bernard. He flicked a switch, and the lights turned off, plunging the room into darkness.

"This again?" Ruby asked.

She received no response. Light elevator music began to play. She seemed to be rising upwards. She clutched the paper in her hands, wondering when her memories would vanish.

They didn't.

The elevator ground to a sudden halt, shaking as something heavy crashed on top of it. The doors didn't open, and the lights flickered and trembled before going out again, plunging Ruby back into darkness.

*I think something went wrong with the rebirth,* she thought to herself. *Oh, great.*

## CHAPTER 4

# Subulo is Terrible at Disguises

Jack watched as Subulo set about attempting to stuff an elevator into the trunk of his minivan.

"I don't think that will fit," Jack said.

"A brilliant observation," Subulo said. "I hadn't noticed that before. See, this is why I chose you to accompany me."

"Oh, shut up," Jack grumbled. "What are you even planning to do with the girl? Rudy, or whatever her name is."

"Shouldn't *Ruby* be an easy enough name to remember?" Subulo asked. "Anyways, I require her specialized talents for things that are not of your concern."

"Couldn't you just open the elevator and transport the girl instead?" Wesley asked.

"No," Subulo said. "For everyone's safety, I'm not going to let her out until we reach our intended destination."

"Yeah, speaking of that," Wesley said. "Where exactly do you even plan on taking us?"

"I'm taking you to the lovely Golden Gateway Academy," Subulo said. "It's a school for the supernaturally gifted."

Jack snickered.

"What's so funny?" Subulo demanded.

"Well, you may have noticed that me and Wesley are neither gifted nor supernatural," he said. "Adding to that, it sounds incredibly lame."

"Let me get this straight," Wesley said. "You want us to go to a school for supernaturally gifted kids or whatever?"

"I think I remember reading about that in a book somewhere," Jack said. "Actually, several books, now that I think about it."

Subulo had given up on shoving the elevator into the trunk and was now instead strapping it to the roof of the car with copious amounts of duct tape. "Well, it's less of a school and more of a re-education center, if you catch my drift. They don't just take supernatural kids; they take the losers, weirdos, and outcasts and turn them into compliant, soulless machines ready to serve their new corporate masters."

"So what exactly differentiates this 'Golden Gateway' from any other public school system?" Jack curiously asked.

Subulo thought for a moment. "Their cafeteria food is slightly better," he finally said. "Alright, I think that'll hold for now."

"Why are we even going to this Golden Gateway in the first place?" Jack asked.

"Jack, I'll humor you," Subulo said. "I'm planning on blowing it up."

Jack's expression must've been pretty funny, because Subulo burst out laughing. "I'm kidding," he said. "It's a pretty average trip, y'know. I'll do some conferencing, pull a few strings, turn some important people against each other before kidnapping them. It'll be great! And then I'll blow it up."

Jack blanched. It occurred to him (not for the first time since meeting Subulo) that he might've made a horrendous mistake in going along with him at all.

Wesley had already climbed into the car. Jack followed suit, doggy-paddling through the air and sliding into the back, anchoring himself to his seat via his seatbelt. He leaned over to Wesley, cupping his hand over his mouth.

"I think we might be riding with a terrorist," he said.

Wesley shrugged. "We can't do anything at this point," he whispered back. "Let's run for it once he lets us out of his sight."

"I can hear you, you know," Subulo said from the driver's seat. "I have awfully good hearing."

Jack felt sweat begin to bead on his brow. "You can?"

"No," Subulo said. "I thought I'd just scare you since you were whispering. Anyways, I don't really care what you were talking about. Hang on tight. Or don't."

He pressed his foot on the gas pedal. The car began to climb upwards, the air transitioning from gelatinous to syrupy to a once again normal consistency. Overhead, a dark, craggy cave ceiling bristled with stalactites, each one large and pointy enough to skewer the minivan.

"Please tell me you don't plan to ram the minivan into those," Wesley said. "Is this going to be a repeat of the tree?"

"Good heavens, no," Subulo said. "What kind of

uncivilized brute would try to exit like that?"

"Well, you entered like that," Jack pointed out. "How exactly do you plan on leaving?"

"It's simple, really," Subulo said. "I'll create a portal, and we'll drive through to Golden Gateway."

"You can do that?" Wesley asked.

"Well, sure," Subulo said. "With some caveats, I'm essentially omnipresent. I've just got to find a suitable candidate for a portal..."

He stroked his chin, glancing around the cavern.

"Wesley, I may have to go back on my word," he said after a moment. "And by may, I mean will."

"Please don't do it," Wesley begged from the back. "Like, I'm pretty sure that you're trying to kill us."

Subulo shrugged. "Well, it's up to you to reassure yourself if that's what you think. Just remember that I'm in the car with you."

The car began to purr, plumes of black smoke rising from beneath the hood.

"Oh, that's not good," Subulo muttered. "Hold on for a second."

He pressed the pedal again. The car made a coughing noise before hesitantly beginning to creep forward. After a moment, the wheels seemed to gain traction midair, and the car began moving at a faster pace.

Subulo was halfway to the nearest stalactite before the engine burst into flames.

"That is definitely not good," Jack said.

"Don't leave the car," Subulo said, hands clenched on the wheel. "Wesley, get your paws off of the handle. You're definitely going to die if you go out now."

Wesley hesitantly slumped back into his seat. The acrid scent of smoke filled the air, making Jack's eyes water as he began to wheeze.

The car sped forward, the stalactite approaching at a dizzying pace. An indistinct image had been imposed upon it, showing the surface of a moonlit lake.

"Hold on tight, people!" Subulo called back. "Let's go in for a water landing!"

*SPLASH.* The minivan's engine began to indignantly splutter as water began to leak into the car. The lavender glow had all but vanished, leaving only the silver light of the moon. Subulo's portal hadn't been perfect; in fact, the car was half embedded in the bottom of the muddy lake, the wheels making forlorn squelching noises as Subulo attempted to drive. Jack's seat belt had been jammed shut, and Wesley was desperately attempting to help him, although he was proving to be more of a hindrance.

The lake continued to surge into the van, torrents of water pouring in as Jack desperately attempted to hold his breath. He could see stars begin to wink before his eyes as he finally wrenched the buckle free. He coughed, bubbles frothing in front of his mouth. He paddled towards the surface, disorientedly shaking his head as miniature streams of water poured down his soaked hair. He began to shiver as he came into contact with the cold night air, glancing around him. A breeze had picked up, causing the grass on the nearby shore to sway. They appeared to be next to a forest; upon closer examination, the lake proved to be quite shallow. Schools of silver-finned fish lazily zoomed by as Jack and Wesley trudged to shore, shaking from the cold.

Subulo, meanwhile, lounged on a nearby beach chair, a pair of sunglasses propped up on his face. The elevator was next to him, strands of grayish duct tape billowing in the wind.

"Well, well, well, look who decided to join the party," he said. "Took you long enough."

"I notice that you're conspicuously dry," Jack muttered through chattering teeth.

"Your subpar portal work nearly cost us our lives," Wesley said.

"Nonsense!" Subulo waved a hand. "Although I do admit it was quite entertaining to watch you struggle from afar."

"Why are we even sticking with you?" Jack grumbled.

"It's not like you have any other choice," Subulo said. "At this point, I'm the only one who will help you."

"You call this help?" Jack asked, gesturing at his soaked clothes. "I almost drowned!"

"You almost drowned, but you didn't. That's the key. If I was anybody else, I would've robbed you blind and then eaten you. Now, come come!" he said, gesturing to the elevator. "Let's open this bad boy."

As the two boys watched, Subulo waltzed over to the elevator and slowly wrenched the doors open. A gunshot echoed from within the elevator, and Subulo fell back. A bullet wound in his head spurted out a stream of blood.

A girl stepped out of the carriage, furtively eyeing her surroundings as a pistol trembled in her hands. Wesley and Jack both backed up as her gaze slid onto them.

"Are you his prisoners?" she asked. She appeared to have gone slightly mad.

Jack and Wesley exchanged a glance. Before they could decide on an answer, Subulo stood back up. His suit was now flecked with streaks of blood.

"That was awfully rude," he brightly said. "You should probably drop the guns, Miss. Let's sort this nasty business out on civil terms."

The girl shot Subulo in the head again. This time, he simply sighed. The bullet wedged itself in his head as he turned to face her. Another bullet hit his forehead again. Jack and Wesley lunged to the side as a hailstorm of bullets whizzed over their heads. Soon, Subulo's face was so riddled with holes that it was beginning to resemble a beehive.

The girl hesitantly lowered her pistols.

"Are you quite done yet?" Subulo politely asked. As the girl watched, his flesh seemed to expand outward, forcing out dozens of bullets from his face. Soon, his wounds had been completely mended. "Bullets don't really work on me. Come to think of it, weapons in general don't really work, either. Are we ready to talk now?"

The girl sighed. "Sure, I suppose," she said. "It's not like this day can get any worse."

Subulo clapped his hands together. "Excellent!" he said. "What I want from you is quite simple. We're at a place called Golden Gateway Academy, a little ways off from the main campus. There's a headmaster here, his name's Alin Antiga."

Subulo paused.

"I want you to kill him."

There was a moment of stunned silence where the boys exchanged nervous looks once more.

The girl simply shrugged. "What do I get in return?"

Subulo smiled. "I'll make all of your worries vanish."

"That's some awfully ambiguous wording," the girl said. "Are there any specifics?"

"I'll pay you enough money for you to live in luxury beyond your wildest dreams," Subulo said. "How about that? I'll trust that you can kill Alin in time."

The girl considered it for a moment, and then nodded. "Couldn't you just do this job yourself?"

"No," Subulo said. "For one, I'm not allowed on the grounds. For another, I don't want to be connected with this in any way whatsoever. Jack, Wesley, this is Ruby. Stay out of her way. I've got different assignments for the two of you."

"Do we have to kill people?" Jack hesitantly asked, eyeing Ruby as she disappeared into the forest.

"No," Subulo chortled. "But you will need a disguise. I'm going to have you both infiltrate the Gateway Convention. For our purposes, it doesn't really matter what it's about. All you need to do is let my man Russell through when he shows up. You'll know when he does. Afterwards, I'll swoop in and extract you all, and we'll have a job well done. Ruby gets paid, and you two get to go home or whatever. Sounds good?"

"Sure, I suppose," Jack said, glancing back at Wesley, who gave a noncommittal shrug. "What choice do we have?"

"Excellent!" Subulo said. "Ready?"

The boys nodded. Subulo took a deep breath and snapped his fingers.

When Jack looked down at himself, he saw that his clothes had dried. Along with that, he was in a new outfit, sporting a rumpled blue button-down shirt with a badge and black tie. The shirt had been messily tucked into a pair of black pants, barely covering his voluminous new potbelly. He also seemed to have gotten taller. He felt around his face. Was that a...mustache?

"What exactly did you do?" he blurted, before covering his mouth in horror. His voice was huskier, deeper. It was as though he had been forcefully shoved into the body of a middle-aged mall cop.

"I disguised you," Subulo said with a wink. "Pretty self explanatory, in my opinion. You are now a security guard, hired for the Gateway Convention."

He held out a mirror for Jack, who found it disconcerting to be staring at someone who was so blatantly not him.

"I'm an old man," Jack said, with no small amount of wonder.

"Yes, and we look exactly the same," Wesley said. "Subulo,

could you at least try to make us look visually distinct?"

Jack looked over to see what was essentially a carbon copy of what he saw in the mirror; a balding old man with a gray mustache, rumpled blue button-down, and black pants, who seemed to mirror his expression of baffled confusion.

Subulo sighed. "So demanding," he muttered, snapping his fingers again.

Wesley's shirt was now white. Nothing else had changed.

Wesley looked back into the mirror. "Well, that's not quite what I meant."

"Enough preparation," Subulo said. "It's time to infiltrate!"

He shepherded the two boys into the elevator, forcing the doors shut and plunging them into darkness. After what seemed like an eternity of listening to their own nervous breathing, the lights flickered to life, the doors opening into a hallway.

Wesley and Jack's eyes went wide as they stepped out of the elevator, surveying the almost distasteful decadence surrounding them.

They had stepped onto a landing overlooking a large dance hall, with twin staircases descending downwards on either side of it. The walls were paneled in golden arcs, modeled to resemble crashing waves. The floor was tiled in white marble flecked with gold. Men in opulent suits played darts and sipped champagne while women dressed in silk and pearls tittered and laughed as they chatted amongst one another. Jazz music softly wafted through the air as a band played nearby. More…exotic sights were there, too; Jack saw a red-skinned man with a pair of prodigious horns standing in line for the buffet, a small, winged, goblin-like creature chugging a bottle of wine, and a woman with a scaly tail trailing outwards from behind her dress swaying to and fro on the dance floor, to name a few. In fact, now that Jack listened, he could hear some distinctly otherworldly vocals on the jazz song that was playing, being sung in a French-like language which didn't sound like it was meant to be spoken by humans.

"I've never seen so much wealth in one party," Wesley marveled.

"I don't get invited to parties," Jack sourly said. "Where does Subulo want us to go? We're not exactly going to blend in here. I think we'd get kicked out for not having enough money."

Just then, to their right, a pair of gilded double doors swung open, an old man in black robes sweeping in. Before Jack or Wesley could find anywhere to hide, he'd grabbed Jack by the shoulders.

"Ah, security!" he said enthusiastically. "Why exactly are you intruding upon my party? If you can't give me a good reason, I'll have you dismembered."

## CHAPTER 5

# Eve Resists the Urge to Make a Pun About 'Chilling Out'

Evening Star was immensely bored. What was the point of owning an entire casino if she couldn't even gamble once in a while?

She observed the comings and goings of the casino deep underground through a series of blinking computer monitors. Data was gathered from the time a die hit the top of a table to each individual pull of a slot machine lever, a series of ones and zeros flowing into a separate data bank connected to Evening's executive room.

However, the executive room was still boring. The concrete floor was littered with dust bunnies, and the room seemed to be permeated with the unshakable scent of dirt and sweat that always lurked in underground places. The endless harsh light of the computer monitors was beginning to hurt her eyes. She'd been spending several days in a row down in the room, and had given up on sleep long ago. She hunched over her keyboard, fingers swiftly clanking out messages to colleagues and fellow members of her gang, The Wolves' Den.

Yes. She was in a gang, although she was more of a

secretary than a gangster. She mostly managed financial transactions, along with the occasional contracted murder.

Eve sighed and pushed away from her desk with her feet, running a hand through her matted and tangled hair as her other hand rubbed her eyes.

Eve looked around the room. On the left wall, her laptop rested on top of her small black desk, dwarfed by the two large pillars of computer monitors which stood on either side of it. The pile of energy drink cans and discarded ramen cup wrappers which huddled in the corner of the room had grown to roughly the size of a small horse. In the opposite corner, a mattress had been thrown upon the floor, blankets and pillows merging together to form a singular fluffy blob.

Eve sighed again and shut her eyes tightly, a wave of drowsiness overcoming her. She yawned, loudly, stretching her arms.

"I should probably take a shower," she said to the pile of garbage.

The pile seemed to shift, as if nodding assent.

Eve had opted for having a bathroom. She tended to appear off-putting to the clients of the casino, and felt that coming up to the ground floor every time she needed to use the loo was a gigantic waste of time.

Eve rose from her chair, stepping into the bathroom. It was clean and orderly, in stark contrast to the chaotic mess that was simultaneously her kitchen, bedroom, and workplace. Eve's toothbrush and toothpaste had been placed perfectly parallel to her soap bar, the tops perfectly aligned.

The white tiles gleamed and shone in the light of a large camping lantern, placed next to the mirror. Although the room was cramped, She made the most of the space. Eve had seen broom closets more roomy than her bathroom.

"Oh, right," she muttered to herself. "I forgot that there wasn't a shower in here."

She undressed and ran a flowery white towel under the faucet before scrubbing herself off with it, warm water dripping onto the tile floor.

Eve looked around and whistled a cheerful tune. The bathroom gave no reply, and she stopped whistling.

Eve hung the towel up on a nearby hook, pulling her pajamas back on. She was on her fifth pair of them, as the rest had started to stink. She probably should've had a washing machine installed in the room.

As Eve walked back into her office and sunk into her chair, a telephone on the desk began to ring. She regarded it blearily before picking up the receiver.

"Hello, Evening Star here," she mumbled, glancing at her power-points.

The voice on the line crackled with static.

"Hello, I'm the clerk for this shift," the voice said. It was a man's voice, deep and resonant. "Ms. Star, a man is here to see you. Are you receiving visitors?"

Sigh.

"Y-yes," Eve said, laughing nervously. "Just give me a minute to…change, alright? You can send him down now."

"Wonderful!" the voice seemed delighted. The phone

line went dead, the earpiece playing a flat dial tone.

Eve put down the telephone. She studied it. It was sleek and black, the light from the fluorescent panels glinting off of its shiny plastic surface.

Eve then realized two things. She didn't have any male clerks, and she'd never brought a telephone down to the room.

Eve whirled around to look at the phone again.

She wavered a bit before picking up the handset. Before she could punch in a number, a voice blared out from the earpiece.

"Hello," the voice said. It sounded faintly gleeful. "This is the front desk at..."

"Fool me once, shame on you," Eve spat. "Who are you? What have you done with the actual clerk?"

The voice paused for a second.

"Well, the clerk for this hour seems to have called in sick. As for who I am, well, how about you come up and find out?"

"Nice strategy," Eve said. "How stupid do you think I am?"

"Not stupid at all," the voice said placatingly. "I'm just trying to conduct negotiations with you in a civilized manner. It's either you come up here or I come down there. Unfortunately, I have quite an aversion to underground places."

"Poor you," Eve dryly said. "What do you plan to do with me once I come up? Kill me? Hold me for a ransom?"

"No," the voice said. "I don't like meaningless death, and I have enough money to spare."

"Then what do you want? I'm sure you didn't come here to make small talk."

"That would be nice, but you're unfortunately correct. I have some requests to make of you," the voice sighed.

"I see," Eve said. "What do I get out of this?"

"A favor from me," the voice said.

Eve snorted. "I don't need anything from you."

"Would knowing who I was change things?" the voice asked.

"Probably not," Eve said. "Let's hear your name."

"Not so fast," the voice said. "I wouldn't want you to get scared and back out before I can ask for my favors."

"And I'm assuming you'll want me to come to you unarmed?" Eve asked.

"Of course not!" the voice exclaimed. "Even if I told you to, you'd still find a way to fit a knife in your boot or something. Bring whatever you want, and I'll try to convince you to not kill me."

"You make an interesting case, stranger," Eve said, already contemplating how she'd murder him. "I'll be up in a minute."

She put down the phone and hastily stepped out of her pajamas and jumped into a wrinkled pair of blue jeans and a bright green t-shirt before frantically clambering into a pair of sneakers. She checked her breath and ran a comb through her hair as she holstered a pistol. She walked to the stainless steel door that marked the exit to her lair, extracting a ring of jingling keys from the mountain of energy drink cans. She fumbled with one of the keys before she unlocked the door with it, wincing as the door screeched open on rusty hinges.

Light spilled out onto a dingy catwalk, the smell of mildew intensifying as Eve stepped out of the room.

Eve's sneakers clanked on the catwalk as she strode towards the stairs, humming a tune while she fiddled with the trigger on her pistol. She reached the door to the stairway.

As she opened the door, a blast of cold air-conditioning hit her squarely in the face, a frigid blast of wind in great contrast to the warm, stuffy underground. The scent of alcohol carried on the draft, washing away the musty scent of Eve's office.

Eve shivered and gritted her teeth, clambering up the staircase with her pistol in hand. As she ascended, the air seemed to get even colder, the temperature plunging with each step she took. By the time she'd gotten to the ground floor of the casino, the floor was no longer visible, blanketed under a chilly white cloud of fog. She waded through the fog.

"It feels like a freezer in here," she muttered, her breath steaming in the air. She drew her shirt in on herself, the cold seeping into her bones as she advanced.

The clerk's desk was predictably empty. Eve checked the security monitor, but the cameras were all off-line, black bars of static crackling on the screen.

Eve checked the desk drawer and found a folded black overcoat, gratefully swaddling herself in it before she plunged on into the casino.

She found her corpse of the day at the slot machines. It was an old man, frozen solid in the act of pulling the lever. His eyes were glazed over, his skin taking on a pale and clammy sheen.

"Wonderful," Eve muttered. "Is his plan to just let me wander around until I freeze to death?"

"Well, it's a little hard to talk to somebody when they're dead, Miss," a voice from behind her said.

Eve spun around and lashed out with her leg, kicking the person behind her directly in the crotch. The man doubled over with a grunt of pain as Eve yanked out her pistol, pressing the gun to his head.

"What do you want?" she demanded. "You'd better speak before I put a bullet through your head."

"Why would you do that?" The man asked, raising his head. He had a shaggy long mane of white hair, his strangely iridescent eyes glinting with malice. His thin lips had stretched into a smile, as though he thought the prospect of imminent death was absolutely hilarious.

"You've turned this joint into a meat locker," Eve snarled. "Surely you have a good reason."

"Well, I do have a good reason, but I wasn't the one to turn your casino into the winter wonderland you see before you," the man chuckled. "That would be Russell's fault."

Eve frowned. "You've got a friend with you?"

The man simply winked at her. "You'll see. Russell! Come he..."

Eve forced the gun against the man's temple. "Are you trying to tag team me?"

"Look, if I wanted to kill you, I would've done so already," the man said, reaching out and snatching the pistol from Eve's hand. As she watched in astonishment, he broke it in half in his fist, flinging the pieces away.

"There," he said. "Now we can talk without me worrying about you shooting me. It would be incredibly inconvenient for me if you happened to do that. I hope you didn't bring a second gun with you, otherwise this would be terribly awkward."

Eve leapt backwards, keeping her distance from the man.

The man shrugged and then grinned. "And speaking of terribly awkward...Russell!"

The fog pooling around them billowed upwards, obscuring the man from view. Eve squinted, focusing on the man's shape in the fog. As she watched, a dark silhouette rose from the ground, stepping up next to the man. The fog dropped like a stage curtain, revealing the smiling man and a new one, a man with a head of tousled blonde hair and a viking-esque beard. The blonde man was clad in a brown fur coat, two hand axes strapped to the leather belt he was wearing.

The man smiled under his beard, his blue eyes twinkling. "Hello," he said, "I'm Russell."

"On the topic of introductions," the other man broke in. "I'm Subulo."

Eve narrowed her eyes. "So I'm in company with the most wanted criminal on the face of this planet...and a blonde Santa Claus?"

"I'm going to take that I'm not the blonde Santa Claus," Subulo said, ignoring Russell's expression. "Well, it is true that I am the most wanted criminal in this world, and several other worlds as well. But I've put that past behind me. I've discovered that the greatest joy that one can have is through helping others. Also, I'm technically obligated to help you, as a punishment."

"A punishment? Who was powerful enough to punish you?" Eve asked incredulously.

Subulo shrugged. "Well, I desecrated a couple of temples during ancient times, and then got a goddess on my tail. Brooke, I think? I hard to remember. I hear she's painting watercolors and smoking cigarettes now. What a laugh! Anyways, she shot me in the back with a wooden arrow, and then made it sprout inside me. Quite painful, and the wood now controls my every move. If I so much as think about killing you, the arrow will sprout even more."

"I would express sympathy, but even I know desecrating a temple is a big no-no," Eve said. "Why exactly would you do that?"

Subulo shrugged. "The thrill of it? For laughs? I don't know. Don't bother asking. I was weird and irrational back then."

"It looks to me like you still are," Eve muttered.

"What was that?" Subulo asked, cupping a hand to his ear.

"Nothing," Eve quickly said. "So you won't be able to harm me?"

Subulo solemnly shook his head. "Not a finger will be laid upon you by me. With that out of the way, are we ready to talk?"

Eve sighed and stood up. "Alright. I'm unarmed, and I'll hope that the arrow holds you in check. Assuming that you're even telling the truth, and that there is an arrow inside you at all."

Subulo shrugged. "I mean, do you want to see the wound? I haven't figured out how to close it yet, but…"

"No, I'm good," Eve hurriedly said. "What do you want from me?"

"Let's talk at the bar," Subulo said. "My best friend is waiting for me there."

"Who's your best friend?" Eve asked.

"Alcohol," Subulo said, winking.

They sat at the bar. Eve sipped on apple cider while Subulo drank wine. Russell had busied himself with mixing together every alcoholic beverage that was readily available into a giant drinking horn, which he'd unslung from his back.

Subulo put down his wine and looked at Eve. "Alright, let's get down to business," he said. "I'm currently escorting some children to Golden Gateway Academy, and would like to enlist your protection once they arrive. If you keep them alive for the entire duration of their stay, you'll receive my praise and endless thanks, along with a fat sack of money."

"Money isn't everything, Subulo," Eve chided. "Time is

much more valuable, and this sounds like a gigantic waste of mine. What's there to worry about if you're escorting them?"

"Well, I just thought that I'd undergo lobotomy and watch paint dry for the rest of my life," Subulo sarcastically said. "It's a waste of my time, too. I'm a busy man, Evening. I guess man isn't the right word. I'm a busy immortal demon, Evening. I'm literally existing in two places at once in order to have this conversation with you, and you won't even give me the time of day."

"Impressive as that sounds, I have better things to do right now," Eve said. "Now, get out of my casino."

Subulo sighed. "Can you at least convince Seguine to go to the Gateway Convention?"

"Um…Gateway Convention?" Eve asked. "I'm kind of new to this whole thing," she sheepishly added, upon glancing at Subulo's expression.

"I can tell," he dryly said. "Well, Gateway Conventions are gigantic wastes of time where old men argue about things that aren't important for a couple of hours. It's like politics, except that these old men are each capable of single handedly destroying an entire nation."

"There's a point to make that that's exactly what politics are, but we'll leave it," Eve said. "Why do you need Seguine there?"

"He hasn't shown up in a long time," Subulo said. "I need to take him in for questioning about a myriad of things, all of which are none of your business."

Eve frowned. "Couldn't you just arrest him or something?"

"Well, I could, but that's not my job. Also, I'm trying to prevent collateral damage by isolating him."

"How ironic," Eve said, gesturing around the building. "How many people have you frozen to death in this building alone? Along with that, you're the most wanted criminal that currently exists. How many innocents have you killed in total? Can you even count them?"

Subulo shrugged. "Psh. Nobody's dead in this building. They'll all thaw eventually, possibly with a mild case of the shivers but none the worse for wear. As for how many people I've killed, I can count them on one hand. Actually, I only need one finger."

"You've only killed one person?" Eve asked.

"Yep," Subulo said. "Death doesn't really serve my purposes terribly well."

"I suppose your plan could work," said Eve. "But how would I convince him to go there?"

"Tell him that you've wanted to go to California for a long time. He loves convenience, and he might take the bait and go along with you. But don't make it too obvious. If he asks what you need to do, just say that you're enjoying the sights. If everything goes smoothly, you'll be safely hidden away from him. Any other member of this gang probably couldn't simply ask to go to California and get to go there, but you have an incredible amount of leverage over him as his surrogate daughter."

Eve blanched. "I can't just play my status as a card, Subulo. It's just not the right thing to do."

"The gangster is going to lecture me on morality," Subulo

said. "You're not exactly the shining paragon of virtue. Just do this for me and you'll be handsomely rewarded for it."

Eve sighed. "Well, whatever," she said. "I suppose I could do with the extra cash, and going to California doesn't sound too bad."

"That's the spirit," Subulo said. "One more thing. If you ever see me again, just shoot me in the face and run in the opposite direction."

Eve frowned. "What?"

"It's complicated. There's this…guy who's trying to kill me, who also happens to be me."

"How does that even work?" Eve asked.

"Like I said, it's complicated," Subulo said. "His name's Croweley, and he's essentially just a manifestation of the worst parts of me. He's got a veritable bouquet of assorted quirky traits, chiefly among them the insatiable desire to kill."

"Sounds like a real charmer," Eve muttered. "Why does he exist, exactly?"

"I don't actually know," Subulo conceded. "I don't think he does, either. He has this whole delusion that killing me and everyone that I've been in contact with will cause him to vanish, somehow. I've tried telling him it won't work, but he's beyond reason at this point. Watch your back, your front, watch anywhere that's susceptible to stabbing, really."s

"Great," Eve said. "Any tips on how to deal with him?"

"He doesn't like knock-knock jokes," Subulo said. "That's about it, really."

"Well, thanks for the help," Eve sarcastically said. "I'll

be sure to keep this ever-helpful advice in mind as Croweley turns my head into a steaming pile of mush."

"Any time," Subulo said, rising from the bar. "Russell, we're heading out," he said, making a waving gesture towards the buff man. "Later, skater." He winked at Eve as thick tendrils of mist began to curl up from the floor. A thin layer of ice formed on the top of Eve's cider as the temperature dropped, the fog filling the room before vanishing.

Eve eyed the patch where Subulo used to be before letting out a despondent sigh.

"This might be the worst decision that I've made since I decided to talk to Subulo," she said. "What've I gotten myself into?"

## CHAPTER 6

# Eve Spectacularly Fails to Stay Alive for More Than One Chapter

Eve had gotten to the heart of her gang in a leisurely ten minute walk.

She'd gained an audience with Seguine, the gang's kingpin, with bizarre ease. She'd strolled up to his building, past several groups of heavily armed guards who regarded her with thorough disinterest, and simply opened the door to his office, which was unlocked. She was convinced that his usual daily routine entailed sitting in his chair and smoking a mind-bogglingly large number of imported Cuban cigars, only stopping for a lunch that consisted of several helpings of whiskey and an especially deep breath.

She caught him the middle of a smoke which didn't surprise her. She regretted not knocking on the door, as he seized a nearby revolver from a desk drawer and had it aimed at her face before she could even take a step into the room.

"Oh, it's Evening," Seguine said, stowing the pistol back into the drawer and going back to his cigars. His antique golden cigar cutter flashed in the light of the overhead lights. Eve had fond memories of when he'd first shown it to her as a child and she'd proceeded to almost cut her index finger off. She had a sneaking suspicion that the incident had something to do with Seguine's decision to serve all of her subsequent meals with plastic forks and knives. "What do you want?"

"I want you to quit smoking," Eve experimentally said, stepping into the velvet-carpeted office. She'd been in the room many times, memorizing almost every detail. Bullet holes marred the wall, relics from gunfights long since fought. The creme-colored wallpaper was covered with floral patterns, roses and daisies intertwining in abstract swirls as they climbed up the walls. Overhead, a slightly broken wooden ceiling fan made a half-hearted attempt at producing a breeze, barely managing the beginnings of a feeble gust. Seguine's wastebasket was nearly filled to the brim with cigar stubs, with important-looking documents crumpled into balls scattered here and there throughout. Seguine was in his favorite desk chair, a towering leather behemoth which seemed more like a throne than a simple chair.

Seguine had almost choked on his cigar with laughter, and was busily coughing up a storm. "Nice try," he managed. "What do you really want?"

"Well, I do want you to quit, but that's not what I'm here for. I want you to go to the Gateway Convention."

Seguine sighed as he lay the cigar down nearby. "Well, now this is unusual. Evening, do you know why I stopped going to the convention?"

Eve shrugged. "You didn't like the people?"

"Well, close enough," Seguine said. "The organizer, Alin, threatened to have me tried in court for fraud, human rights abuses, money laundering, etcetera, if I didn't help him force a vote."

Eve winced. "Ouch," she murmured.

Seguine swiveled his chair around to face her. He was wearing a pair of gold-rimmed tea shades, his bald pate glistening with sweat. His scent, an acrid combination of tobacco smoke and alcohol, seemed to hang over the room like a heavy cloud. He was wearing a Hawaiian button-up shirt, the kind that a tourist would wear, blue fabric patterned with parrots and coconuts; it rather ruined the intimidating effect which he seemed to be going for. "Why exactly did you ask me for this favor, Evening?"

"Call it a whim," Eve casually said, hoping that her expression didn't give away the lie. "I've always wanted to know what happens during those meetings."

Seguine massaged his forehead. He appeared to be thinking. Finally, after a suitably lengthy pause, he glanced back up.

"It's not like I have anything better to do," he muttered. "If it's really what you want, I guess I can go."

Eve blinked. "Really? Simple as that?"

"Were you expecting more resistance?" Seguine asked. "I'm not terribly anxious to remain at home. And if I'm going to go, I've got a few matters that I'd like to discuss at the convention, as well. Go before I change my mind."

The rest of the building was in great contrast to Seguine's

office, with white linoleum flooring and flickering industrial light panels loosely scattered across the ceiling. Combined with the chilly air conditioning, Eve got the eerie sensation that she was standing in a morgue. She managed to wave at the guards on her way back into the elevator, who regarded her with the same amount of disinterest as they'd shown her before.

Eve stepped into the lobby of the building. It was quiet and empty at this time of night, save for a man with a shaggy white head of hair who was sitting at the front, humming a song as he propped his legs up on the secretary's desk.

"Greetings, Eve," he said, tossing her a roguish wink.

"What are you doing here, Sub..." Eve began.

"Shh," Subulo said. "Call me Rob."

"Ok then, Rob," Eve said. "What are you doing here?"

"Well, you need a taxi, right? I'm here to offer. No need to thank me." Subulo took his legs off of the desk and stood up, brushing his pants off.

"Why?" Eve asked.

"Well, to be frank, I wasn't even sure that you'd take me up on my offer," Subulo apologetically said.

"So you're here to ensure that I don't flake out on you?" Eve asked.

Subulo shrugged. "Basically. Why don't we go to the taxi? I think I hear Seguine coming."

Subulo stretched and then yawned, pushing the door open with his foot as he ambled outside. As Eve stepped out of the building, she realized that it was raining, fat drops of water angrily splattering against the sidewalk.

"Here you are," Seguine's voice said from behind her. "Let's go. Is the taxi ready?"

Eve turned to see that Seguine was now wearing an oddly bulky trench coat, which made metallic noises with each step that he took.

"Yes," Eve replied, gesturing to Subulo's taxi. "What's with the getup?"

Seguine put a finger to his lips, his teashades glinting menacingly.

Subulo walked up to Seguine, his mouth stretching into a grin. "Hello, good sir," he said. "May I take your bags for you?"

"Of course, thank you," Seguine politely said. "After you, Evening."

"Thanks," Eve said, stepping into the taxi.

Seguine crammed himself into the seat next to her, his head uncomfortably scraping against the ceiling as he hunched over.

"I hate taxi ceilings," Seguine groaned. "Terrible for my back."

"Sometimes I wish that I was as tall as you," Eve said. "And then there are these times."

"Don't worry," Subulo said from the front. "We'll be at the airport in no time, Mister."

Rain splattered on the taxi's roof as Subulo drove downtown. Subulo turned on the radio, fiddled with the knob, then turned the radio off again.

Eve stared out the window at the sky. New Orleans passed by in a dull gray blur as Subulo drove,

Just when Eve thought that she could no longer stand to sit in the taxi any more, Subulo pulled up in front of the Lakefront Airport.

"That'll be…$24.76, good sir," Subulo said.

Seguine fumbled around in his wallet before paying with two twenty dollar bills. "Keep the change," he said. "Let's go, Evening."

Eve looked back at Subulo as she pulled out her luggage from the trunk. He was drumming his fingers on the steering wheel, gazing at the sky.

She pulled the trunk shut and entered the airport, jogging towards Seguine's retreating figure. She caught up to him as they walked away from the check-in lines, heading towards the emergency exit.

"Where are we going?" Eve asked curiously.

"Did you think that we'd be going through security?" Seguine asked, lowering his teashades with his hand. "I'm carrying my body weight's worth in weapons, Evening. We're taking a charter plane. It will be ready for you at any time."

"Thanks, Seguine," Eve said. "But why are you carrying so many weapons? Wouldn't they just slow you down?"

Seguine shrugged, making a loud *CLUNK* as several objects shifted under his coat. "They might, but they'll prove useful later," he said. "Anyways, help me disable the emergency alarms. We're going to have to take the fire exit to the runway."

"Won't people see us climbing down the fire exit?" Eve asked.

"Eve, the thing is, we as a species are predisposed to not care about things that don't pertain directly to ourselves," Seguine said. "If we act like we belong in a place that we don't, others will assume that we do belong. And if not, we'll just have to run really fast."

"That's a pretty stupid plan," said Eve.

"Do you have a better one?" asked Seguine.

"No," Eve conceded. "I'll get to work on the alarm."

She fumbled around the panel of the fire alarm, connecting wires with duct tape as she braced herself for imminent failure.

"You do know how alarms work, right?" Seguine asked, looming behind her.

"Who doesn't?" Eve asked. "If the door is opened, the circuit is opened, and the current stops flowing. Blah blah blah, alarm sounds, we get arrested."

"Excellent," Seguine said. "Remember, if we get caught, just know that it'll be your fault for messing up the wiring."

"Wow, I'm really feeling the love here," Eve muttered. "Get going. I'm right behind you."

Seguine shuffled noisily across the doorway, hesitantly climbing down a rusty ladder to the runway. A white jet was idling nearby, engines rumbling.

As soon as she'd finished duct-taping the wires together, Eve sprinted across the doorway, vaulting over the ladder and rolling onto the runway.

"Showoff," Seguine said. "Save your energy."

"Pfft. I have enough to spare," Eve said. "I've been cooped up for too long in that accursed executive room."

"Fair enough," Seguine said. "But you should probably act more normal now, before people begin to stare. People are never that energetic at an airport. They're either a half-asleep, caffeine-deprived shell of a person, or they're a young child. There's no in-between."

Eve sighed. "Ugh. Airports suck."

"That's the spirit," Seguine said, strolling towards the idling jet plane.

~

Eve really hated plane rides.

She'd sat down, lain back in her cushioned chair, and was drifting into a peaceful sleep before a bone chilling scream pierced the silence, startling her out of her chair and introducing her face-first to the floor.

"Seguine, did you murder the pilot?" she called.

"No," Seguine replied from the seat behind her. "Someone's in the plane with us."

"Oh, ok," Eve said. "I love unexpected visitors."

She crouched behind her seat and pulled out her pistol.

The intercom crackled. "Good afternoon, lady and gentleman. I'm...what's my name again? Never mind. More importantly, your flight to California will begin quite shortly. We'll be landing in Golden Gateway and killing everyone, and you both will help me. Once I figure out how to start this thing, we'll be on our way! Hoo hoo, make sure to not die!"

The plane's engine began to rev as more mad cackling came over the radio, pitched and distorted with static.

Seguine rolled his eyes behind his teashades. "I guess it's amateur hour over here," he muttered. "Let's kill this fool, Evening."

"You don't have to tell me twice," Eve said. "But hasn't he locked the doors to the cockpit?"

"Way ahead of you." Seguine rushed to the cockpit's entrance and reared back his fist. In one blow, he punched a hole straight through the reinforced steel.

He dispassionately examined his knuckles, which had begun to swell. "This looks big enough for you to climb through, Evening," he said, gesturing at the hole.

"Ah, yes. I'd love to slowly wiggle through a small hole whilst at the complete mercy of what ever is on the other side."

"Geez, so demanding," Seguine sighed. "I'll punch the door again."

"I wouldn't do that if I were you," the intercom blared. "We're lifting off, and I only need one of you two. Don't test my patience. I actually don't have patience. So sit down."

The plane suddenly reared forward like a pouncing cat, sending Eve and Seguine sprawling. The plane barreled across the runway, upending racks of luggage and trailing sparks. It soared upwards, reaching speeds that shouldn't even have been possible.

"Now this is a plane ride!" the intercom cried. "I hope you didn't vomit all over the place."

Seguine now had a look of mild annoyance upon his face. "He's really getting on my nerves. He sounds…familiar. Well, no matter."

Seguine slightly loosened his trench coat, causing several grenades to noisily spill onto the floor of the plane. He picked a cylindrical canister, examining it before nodding with satisfaction, ignoring Eve's expression of tangible horror. He pulled the pin, silently lobbing it through the hole as it began to hiss.

The intercom crackled. "What the…"

There was an audible hiss as thick plumes of gray smoke billowed from the cockpit.

"A smoke grenade? Really? I hope you bozos understand that I'm piloting the plane. If I can't see, then we all blow up."

Seguine rolled up the sleeves of his coat, cracking his knuckles before he launched himself at the door again. Steel shrieked as he punctured the door. There was a squeal of pain on the intercom.

"Oh, that's low," the voice moaned. "Not the crotch, if you mind. Actually, you know what? This is less fun than I thought. I'm outta here."

Silence. The intercom blared static.

"Eve, he's vanished," Seguine said, climbing back through the ruined wreckage of the cockpit entrance. "I'll be piloting the plane now."

"I'm going to assume that you know how to fly a plane," Eve said.

"Probably. Maybe. I hope so," Seguine said, ducking back into the cockpit.

"Well, that was over quickly," Eve muttered, sinking back into her chair. There was something she'd forgotten to mention to Seguine, but the thought eluded her mind. There would be time to discuss it once they landed in California. She began to close her eyes, feeling the lolling currents of sleep begin to wash her away from shore.

Something cold and sharp abruptly slashed across her neck. Eve's eyes flew open, and she saw blood dripping across her shirt front. She attempted to scream for help, but could only make vague spitting noises as a thick vermilion river began to pour from her mouth. Someone was waving a knife in front of her face. Her eyes widened still as she saw who it was.

It was Subulo, but it wasn't. He had the same white hair and strange iridescent eyes, but upon his face was a hideously blank smile. It was somehow intensely emotionless; it was as though the muscles making the face contort and stretch had read a book on how to smile, but hadn't quite gotten to the chapter discussing why a smile was made.

Eve coughed. Her mouth was thick with the taste of her own blood. The man's smile grew wider, and his knife came up for the final slash.

Eve managed one final, guttural sigh before the blade plunged home. She had time to see the handle embedded through her throat before her vision grew foggy and indistinct, her breath sputtering out like a dying flame before going out completely. As her vision faded, she heard Seguine shout from the cockpit as the plane suddenly tilted to the side, the nose dipping down as it began to plunge down towards the Earth. In her last moments, she heard the loud *CRUNCH* of metal as the plane collided with something, the cockpit screeching in pain as it was crushed like a tin can in a garbage compactor. Eve could hardly even muster the strength to care as she drifted to her death.

And yet, as she died, she could hear something beckoning from the void, a scrap of consciousness that floated into her outstretched hands from the soot-black river of Death.

Was that...elevator music?

## CHAPTER 7

# Several Immortal Degenerates Bicker in a Dining Room

Alin regarded the two hired guards with disdain. Although he had went all-out in appointing a lavish party, he had skimped on the security spending. He supposed that it wasn't amiss for them to assume that the party was the Gateway Convention, but he wouldn't have time to direct them back to their posts.

The two guards seemed to have frozen in fear, identical expressions of fear on their pudgy, walrus-like faces as their paintbrush mustaches indignantly quivered.

Alin narrowed his eyes. "Are you two related or something?"

The guards nodded their heads, although they still seemed to be incapable of forming coherent words. Alin sighed.

"Look, we're short on time," he said. "Your posts are down this hallway. A black booth next to the gate. Check the guest list before letting anyone through. You've done this before, I assume. Off you go."

He brushed past the security guards, checking his watch. He had sacrificed precious seconds better spent elsewhere.

The convention was about to start, and Alin had enough problems to deal with as is. The plumbing had been malfunctioning, the teachers were going on strike, and the Lovecraftian horrors lurking in the school's basement had attempted their twelfth escape of the semester, with Alin barely managing to recapture them all. He wondered why he even hired security guards when anything that would bother attacking the school would either be strong enough to vaporize mortals in milliseconds or stupid enough to be killed by any occupant who happened to be strolling the grounds. He'd consigned the students to their dormitories (and some to their padded cells), but it did little to help the tedious process of organizing the convention itself.

Alin exhaustedly ran a hand through his hair. Much to his annoyance, he found that his body couldn't quite sustain itself after three consecutive sleepless nights. He attempted to push open the door to the side entrance, finding himself stymied for an unreasonably long time before he realized that it was a pull door. He growled in frustration as he stormed into the parking lot, probably scaring away any passersby who happened to catch a glimpse of him. He realized how repulsive he must've looked; a haggard, gaunt old man with dirty silver hair and looming shadows under his eyes, wearing what amounted a glorified black silk bathrobe.

Alin staggered his way across the manicured hedges of his campus, unsteadily lurching through the oaken double doors to his office. He turned into his bathroom, barely making it to the toilet before he promptly emptied the contents of his stomach into the bowl (although there wasn't much in there to begin with). He briefly contemplated smoking opium to relieve his nerves (he had a reserve stashed in a nearby cabinet), although he was almost certain that his lungs would give out. After wiping his mouth with a washcloth, Alin stripped off his disheveled robes into something more presentable (although only comparatively). Soon, he was clad in a red plaid shirt and jeans a size too large, secured with a black leather belt one size too small. He looked like an aging, half-starved lumberjack. His mind had roused itself from its stupor, desperately attempting to restore some semblance of order to his schedule. He checked his watch again. It was five fifty; Alin's VIP guests were slated to arrive at six o' clock.

Alin freshened up with a hard, robotic determination, rubbing the dry, paper-like skin raw with a pumice exfoliation stone mostly intended for feet. He brushed his teeth and flossed (although it was less flossing and more forcibly ramming his gums with a piece of string) so vigorously that his gums began to profusely bleed.

Alin ducked back out of the restroom. He still had one thing to do. He strode over to what could generously be called his bed, which consisted of several Christmas gifts' worth of knitted woolen blankets piled over a large, circular stone slab. Tossing aside the blankets, he dragged the slab into the center of the room, scraping the wooden floorboards and grunting from the effort. After muttering a hurried verse, he reached over to his desk, picking up a large curved knife from amongst piles of unopened letters and paperwork. He carefully made an incision on his palm, drawing blood. As the droplets fell, they hissed on contact with the stone like cold water on a hot surface. The rust-red stains on the slab began to emit a soft reddish glow, casting shadows on the walls of Alin's office.

Alin agitatedly checked his watch again. "I understand that there needs to be some level of ceremony for this, but can we hurry it up?"

The slab seemed to comply. An inkwell and quill emerged from the slab, along with a sheet of fresh parchment paper. The demon seemed to be in a good mood today; the quill usually jammed itself up Alin's nostril upon arrival.

Alin wiped the sweat from his brow and signed the parchment paper, trying not to drip blood on his signature.

The inkwell, quill, and parchment paper abruptly vanished, along with the bloodstains on the slab. Alin lugged the unwieldy thing back to its nest of blankets, arranging the blankets so as to shield the slab from prying eyes. Alin already felt better; his mind had been cleared, his energy had returned, and his headaches had all but dissolved. He even thought that he could do consecutive jumping jacks without breaking his hip. He'd almost forgotten how good it felt to be young again.

Alin checked his watch. It was five fifty eight. He straightened his collar and adjusted his hair one final time.

He turned to his office door and opened it, stepping through into the Gateway Convention's meeting room.

Several pairs of eyes turned to Alin. His guests had all arrived before him.

"Don't tell me I'm late," Alin said.

"No, you're early," one voice called from the back. "We just all happened to arrive earlier than you."

Alin sighed as he remembered how much he despised the Gateway Convention's meetings. He'd had to sign a contract mandating them in order to get funds to build the academy, but he was regretting his decision. The meeting room bugged him. It only opened on the day of the Gateway Convention, and changed its layout each time, going from a science lab to a living room to the inside of a barn. Not only that, but any attempts to redecorate it would invariably cause whatever decorations had been put in place to burst into flames. The rotten icing on the expired cake for Alin was that his guests all insisted on using the room, no matter what form it took. He'd had one particularly awkward Convention where he'd had to hold the meeting in a public restroom complete with smell. On this particular day, it seemed that Alin would be hosting his guests in a picture-perfect recreation of his grandmother's kitchen and dining room, with Mexican ceramic tiled floors, white granite counter-tops, and even the red checkered tablecloth which had been present in every meal of his youth. A veritable horde of cat-shaped salt and pepper shakers grinned at the occupants of the room, which consisted of four people... although *people* was an inaccurate term...gathered around the dining room table. The portal had spit him out right behind one of the chairs, upon which he tripped as he attempted to walk forward.

After he'd brushed himself off and endured the laughter of his guests, Alin consulted the guest list. "I trust you all found your way here fine. Did the security guards give you any grief?"

An Asian man with long dark hair and tan skin snickered as he fiddled with a napkin holder, an abnormally long and purplish tongue lolling out of his mouth. "They seemed to be markedly incompetent," he remarked. "Not that I mind, but where'd you even get those two?"

"I had a friend provide them," Alin mildly said, scanning around the room. "Is everybody here?"

"I think we're missing Seguine," Ibeti said, setting the napkin dispenser down.

"Big surprise," muttered Alin. "I'm going to go ahead and convene the meeting right now. Are there any objections?"

The room was silent.

"Cool," Alin said. "Alright. What did you all want to talk about?"

An elderly man sitting to Ibeti's left coughed into his fist. "Let's talk about budgeting. Alin, you've got to stop spending so much on accommodation for the students."

Alin spoke. "Nanook..."

The old man held up a hand. "Don't use that name. Call me Harrison."

"Harrison," Alin said. "I simply can't stop spending so much until the Eldritch deities are obliterated or otherwise removed from the premises. I've notified you of this, but haven't gotten a response. On top of that, they keep breaking out of their confines and attempting to maul the students, which takes an awful lot of bribery and paperwork to keep quiet."

Harrison shrugged. "I don't terribly mind the spending affair, but do you have a solution for the deities?"

"Well, diplomacy's off the table because we can't communicate, but we're planning to stow them away in a pocket dimension of some sort," he said.

"Pocket dimensions," Ibeti vaguely said, picking up the napkin holder again and toying with it once more. "Eldritch gods. Things got complicated once I moved here and stopped eating fetuses." He looked glum. He slumped down, his movements dull and listless.

"Yeah, but eating fetuses is pretty messed up," a voice piped up. A small chubby boy wearing what looked like a white bed-sheet adjusted it, a pair of white wings uncomfortably sandwiched between him and the back of his chair. "Besides, at least you were feared. I'm a *symbol*."

"But you're depicted everywhere." A man wearing a metal mask in the shape of a wolf's head spoke. "I'm just a folk character. I wasn't even the main character of the stories. Reynard took care of that for me."

Alin let out an internal sigh as the meeting dissolved into petty fighting amongst one another. They were always like this; he'd found that immortals didn't become wiser with age. In fact, from his personal experiences, it was the opposite.

Folk characters grew bitter as the ones who'd remembered them vanished and were forgotten. Spirits and deities who'd grown powerful with worship became gaunt and weak, mere shadows of their old selves. Even the lucky ones who had become mainstream and widely accepted lived in a constant state of fear at the revelation that their days were numbered.

The four continued to bicker amongst themselves while Alin leaned back in his chair, staring at the ceiling in a futile attempt to avoid rolling his eyes.

There was a knock on the door to the meeting room. There was a lull in the conversation as every occupant of the room turned to look at the door in unison.

"Come in," Alin called.

There was no reply. Alin began to shiver as the room's temperature became noticeably colder. A thick curtain of fog rolled over the room, blurring Alin's vision.

"Do you think this is an attack?" the rosy-cheeked, cherub-like boy asked.

"Most likely," Alin said. "You all can defend yourselves, right?"

"Presumably," Harrison huffed. "It feels like home already."

"Right," Ibeti said, clapping his hands together. "I was getting hungry, anyways."

"Everybody shut up," the masked man growled. "He's getting closer."

*BONG.* There was a sound of something hard striking metal. There was a whimper as the masked man's silhouette slumped in his chair, a dark outline appearing behind him.

Ibeti leaped across the table at the outline but missed, nearly smashing his face into the floor. The fog thickened, but Ibeti's voice could be heard through it.

"Hey, is that an axe? Watch where you're swinging that thing. Whoa! Nearly missed me there."

There was a squeal of pain, and Ibeti's voice abruptly stopped. By now, Harrison and the boy had huddled close to Alin, Harrison unslinging an inordinately large wooden bow, nocking an arrow. The boy simply sighed and snapped his fingers, a cigarette appearing in his hand. He stuck it in his mouth and stuck up his index finger, which caught flame and began to burn. He breathed in for longer than seemed necessary, holding his breath. Something began to rumble in the boy's stomach.

Without warning, the boy's body erupted into flames as he began to spew globs of burning ash every which way. After a long moment, the mist thinned by an almost imperceptible amount.

Alin and Harrison stared bug-eyed at the boy, who simply wiped the residual ash off of his mouth and summoned another cigarette. "Well?" he snapped. "I hope that was worth it. Those things burn like you wouldn't believe."

A large, leather gloved hand reached out from the fog and grabbed the little cherub, who indignantly squealed as he was pulled out of view. Harrison cursed, brown patches of fur starting to grow on his face and hands. He rushed into the fog as the beginnings of a snout begun to form. There was a roar, a meaty *THWACK*, and then silence once more. Alin, meanwhile, had busied himself with mentally composing his obituary.

Something large stirred in the fog. Alin shifted to one side, pressing his back against a wall. He could hear the clinking of chain mail as heavy footsteps strode towards him. A presence loomed directly in front of him. Alin swore that he saw metal gleam through the fog. He braced himself for a blow.

The blow never came. The fog rapidly began to thin, revealing an empty room. All four of Alin's guests had vanished, presumably spirited away by the force in the fog. Alin's heart began to beat faster, but he composed himself and stood.

"Fancy meeting you here, Alin."

Alin slowly turned around and was rewarded with a hearty whack to the forehead, knocking him to the floor. An inordinately tall man stood above him, thick curtains of white hair falling downwards as he bent to look at Alin, his eyes gleaming with homicidal glee as he tipped a black top hat.

"You're...Subulo," Alin breathed, backing away. "I thought I banned you for..."

"I'm not Subulo," the man who looked like Subulo breathed. "I'll admit that it's an easy mistake to make. No, no. I'm Croweley."

Alin took a look at the man. Upon closer inspection, Alin could make out a few discrepancies that distanced this doppelganger from Subulo. The man's movements were unnaturally stiff, as though he was a corpse fighting rigor mortis. He was clutching a brown leather suitcase, his hands trembling on the handle. He wore a perverse, corrupted mimic of Subulo's trademark easygoing grin, the expression more akin to one found on the face of someone having their toenails forcibly removed one at a time.

"See it now?" Croweley hissed. "I don't have much time, Alin, so I'll be taking you with me for now. You're my... what's the word? Insurance."

Croweley lurched towards Alin, his hand outstretched.

"No thanks," Alin said, leaping to his feet. "I'll just be going now."

Croweley's eye nervously twitched. "I wasn't asking your permission."

Alin took the high road and punched Croweley in the face, hurting his fist in the process. His flesh was as hard as any metal Alin had come across; it was reminiscent of punching a particularly large fridge.

Croweley sighed and grabbed Alin's throat, beginning to squeeze. His grip was like iron upon Alin's neck, who gasped as his vision swam.

Unfortunately for Croweley, Alin had survived enough assassination attempts to have perfected the art of running away. He attempted to execute one particularly advanced maneuver where he twisted out of his would-be assassin's grasp, only to be met with the unfortunate realization that his neck would break if he attempted to do so. He tried several other techniques upon the same line, only to be stymied by the fact that his neck still counted as a part of his body.

Although Alin had perfected the art of running away, he figured that he could get some practice in the art of begging for his life. He turned to face Croweley as best he could, preparing to speak even as his vocal chords were being ground into piles of meaty flesh.

"Aghhghhh," Alin firmly and deliberately stated. It turns out that begging for one's life was hard when they were being choked to death, although Alin noticed that Croweley didn't know how to properly choke someone. He wasn't attempting to apply pressure to the windpipe; in fact, it looked like he was using a novel new method of instead crushing Alin's neck until he died.

Croweley didn't seem to realize this. He glared at Alin, who spluttered and coughed as he tightened his grip.

Dark splotches appeared in Alin's sight. He could see tiny flecks of light dancing before his eyes. Was this going to be how he died?

As he slipped into the dark depths, he could feel Croweley's grip loosen. He took in a gasping, rattling breath, feeling fresh air enter his lungs. He was saved!

Just as he began to properly appreciate his freedom, Alin hit his head on the tiled floor. Hard.

Although Alin was a tough, cunning man, his body was rather fragile. He was not one to be easily outsmarted or led into a trap, but he, like most other humans, was easily defeated with trauma to the head.

The stars brightened, swallowing his vision whole. Alin took a final, deep breath as he was dragged under the dark current. He felt the world slipping from under him as he floated into the light.

## CHAPTER 8

# Another Subulo Shows Up (One Was Too Many, Frankly)

Jack and Wesley had walked out of the warm confines of the dance hall and were promptly slapped across the face with a sharp blast of freezing wind, piercing directly through their flimsy shirts. Jack rubbed his hands together to warm them up, although they were so numb he felt like he was smashing two rocks together.

"How're you holding up?" he asked Wesley.

"My hands have been stolen and replaced with frozen slabs of tofu," Wesley mumbled.

The boys wandered through the dying, brownish gardens and past the frozen-over fountains in silence; they found they'd lost the energy to speak, settling for letting their mouths erratically chatter like a pair of defunct nutcrackers. They eventually wound their way into the parking lot, making a beeline for the lone guard station. It was a sad sight, a solitary steel booth with a flimsy, red-striped barricade arm barring vehicle access. The inside of the booth smelled faintly of fish and rancid coffee, a combination that sounded about as appealing as it smelled. The linoleum flooring glinted in the light of the dead insect-filled LED ceiling panels. Windows had been placed on all sides of the booth, allowing for full three hundred and sixty degrees view into the endless, pitch-black winter night. A row of televisions and monitors had been tuned to view security camera footage, although their corresponding security cameras all appeared to have been pointed towards walls. Two leather office chairs had been prepared, in which they gratefully sank into.

"It smells gross," Wesley said. "Why'd Subulo make us do this?"

"I guess he's pretty desperate for help," Jack muttered. "Either that, or he's planning to murder us both in this very conveniently isolated space."

There was a moment of nervous silence as both boys glanced around the security booth. Jack eyed the televisions suspiciously, but they seemed safe and Subulo-free, at least for the moment.

Wesley twiddled his thumbs, rolling his office chair next to Jack's. "Is there a guest list?" he asked, peeking over Jack's shoulder.

Jack vaguely gestured to a pile of papers which sat on the desk. "It's probably in there somewhere," he said. "I really can't find the energy to look for it."

Wesley seized the papers and rifled through the stack, drawing out a particularly diminutive index card. Jack would've missed it if he'd been the one looking for it.

"I think this is it," he said, scanning over it with his eyes before passing it to Jack.

"Awfully small, isn't it?" Jack asked, glancing over the

names. There were five people on the list, names inscribed in black ink. "Seguine, Ibeti, Nanook, Ysengrim, Plutto. What's with supernatural folks in weird names?"

"Let me have a look," Wesley said, snatching the card back from Jack's hand. "Why are these guys' names so hard to pronounce? Eye-betty? Yee-sen-grim?"

"Your guess is as good as mine, really," Jack said. "At least we won't have to worry about asking for last names."

A black Mercedes-Benz rolled up in front of the security booth. A man with long, shaggy black hair rolled down the window and stuck his head out, exposing an unusually long purple tongue.

"I'm Ibeti, pronounced *ee-betty*," he rasped, his voice akin to the sound of nails scraping a chalkboard. "I've brought everyone else with me, excluding Seguine."

The passenger window rolled down. An old man with silver hair tied into braids waved from the passenger seat, while a person wearing wolf-shaped metal mask hoisted what appeared to be a cherub up into Jack's view, although neither party looked happy about the arrangement. With the exception of the cherub, who wore a miniature white toga, they had all been dressed in black formal suits. The outfits, combined with their glum expressions, reminded Jack of mourners headed for a funeral.

Ibeti shot Jack an expectant look.

Jack, who'd been frozen with fear, had forgotten to lift the arm. He looked around the booth, pressing any buttons which looked like they would raise the barrier. Instead, he managed to make the lights begin to frantically strobe on and off, activate the coffee machine, which proceeded to spill coffee grounds and water everywhere, and trigger a radio somewhere in the booth, which began to play an easy-listening station at maximum volume. After shooting Jack a look of slightly baffled amusement, Ibeti rolled the window back up. The Mercedes accelerated, passing straight through the barrier as though it didn't exist at all.

"That went well," Jack moaned. "Shut up, Wesley."

Wesley, who had doubled over laughing, halfheartedly held up his hands in protest. "Hey, it went about as expected," he managed. "At least they didn't try to kill you."

Jack sighed. "Weird, huh? What was with that dude's tongue, anyways?"

"Don't ask me," Wesley said. "How many licks do you think it takes for him to finish a lollipop?"

Before Jack could respond to the question, a large, flat sheet of rock sailed through the barrier, cleanly shattering the entire arm. A stocky blonde man clad in chain mail and fur sprinted past the guard booth, not even sparing the boys a glance.

"Do you think that's the person Subulo mentioned?" Wesley asked Jack. "What's his name again? Russell. That's right."

"I sure hope it's Russell," Jack said. "Either that, or we've just let a serial killer in."

"Well, what can you do," Wesley said, leaning back in his office chair. "I guess it really do be like that sometimes."

"Did you just...never mind."

Outside, snow had begun to fall, painting the pavement white.

"Check it out," Wesley whistled. "Snow."

"Yeah, it's almost like it's the winter or something," Jack said.

Wesley snorted. "You have a point," he said. "It's not like we'd get this back home, though."

Jack shrugged. "Fair enough," he said.

They sat in silence, watching the snow fall. The night was peaceful and serene, the silence only broken by the occasional gust of wind. Stars had begun to twinkle in the ink-black sky, pinpricks of light glimmering in the infinite, jet-colored sea. Jack took a moment to marvel at how small he was, a mere grain of sand in the horrifyingly large and unfeeling universe.

"*COWABUNGA!*"

The night sky was abruptly blotted out by a large mass of chain mail. The man who'd broken the barrier, Russell, had paused in front of the security guard's booth, peeking in and knocking on the windows. His knuckles were bleeding, and he'd sustained a black eye. Inexplicable patches of burning black ash appeared to have made themselves at home in Russell's tangled blonde locks.

"It's time to go," Russell said, his breath fogging up the glass.

"I like the hairdo," Jack said. "A bold fashion choice, but I think it works."

Russell sighed. "Yes, yes. I do look like I've been dragged

through a used cigarette repository, but never mind that. Subulo wants us to withdraw."

"Withdraw? We just got here, dude!" Wesley said. "I'm not particularly eager to stay, but are we done that quickly?"

"Yes we are," Russell simply said. "What were you expecting? Kidnapping people isn't something that one drags out. I'd love to chat more about this, but I'm pretty sure that we're being followed."

Russell bent double, coughing. A large wooden spike wriggled its way through the front of his chest, puncturing his chain mail armor. Subulo walked into view, clutching a suitcase in his hand.

"I do despise zombies," Subulo calmly pronounced, pausing in front of the booth to yank an oaken cane out of Russell's body. He turned to face the boys, wiping the cane off on his dress pants. His head and shoulder nervously twitched. His pupils were grotesquely dilated, blocking out the whites of his eyes. "Right. The fun's about to happen now. I can finally live out my centuries-long ambition of ending my suffering, and I'll need you both to do that."

"Hey, I'm starting to get the feeling that isn't Subulo," Wesley whispered to Jack.

"Gee, what tipped you off?" Jack whispered back. "Here's the plan: I push all of the buttons in this booth, scream for help in an incredibly masculine manner, and then we'll both run away. How does that sound?"

"Good to me, assuming he lets us live that long," Wesley responded.

*Not-Subulo* hurled his suitcase through the window, breaking the glass.

Jack and Wesley bolted through the door, their speed only hampered by the fact that they seemed to have inherited the physique of their disguises as well, i.e. crippling arthritis and fat rolls so large they had begun to form their own gravitational fields. Jack, who was an unenthusiastic member of his school's cross-country team, managed to go a bit further than Wesley before his gout-ridden joints forced him to stop. Out of breath, he turned around to see that they'd barely cleared the threshold of the security guard booth.

*Not-Subulo* snickered. "I think you've both had a good run, boys. Well, that run was kind of pathetic, but you get what I mean. How about you cease the foolish resistance and come back to me?"

"Well, we can't exactly come back to you," Wesley panted. "I think I might've pulled a muscle. Several muscles, in fact."

*Not-Subulo* sighed. "This is beneath me," he muttered. "If I wanted to spend my day picking up old men, I'd get my flirt on at the retirement home."

As *Not-Subulo* stooped down to haul Wesley up, a large slab of rock hit him squarely in the head. He collapsed face-first into the parking lot's pavement while Russell ran towards him, yelling like a lunatic. He held a wickedly gleaming ax in each hand, which he promptly used to eviscerate *Not-Subulo's* head, rending his skull into bloody chunks of kibble, pausing only to bellow what sounded like expletives in a language foreign to Jack and Wesley.

After spending longer than seemed strictly necessary on splattering *Not-Subulo's* brain matter across the concrete, Russell wiped his brow with a hand. "Whew," he said, seemingly blind to the boys' twin expressions of terrified nausea. "I really needed that."

Jack unsuccessfully attempted to hold down the contents of his stomach. It was remarkable how much vomit could be produced from a single pastry strudel.

"Russell, could you…avoid doing this in the future?" Wesley retched.

Russell blinked at the boys. He was covered in red, as though he'd tripped while attending a tomato-sauce tasting convention. "Is something wrong?" he asked.

"Well, it's just that we're pretty new to this whole violent murder business," Wesley said, his face a light shade of green.

"And I thought the hell-hound was nasty," Jack muttered, wiping his mouth. "That was grody, Russell. I'm pretty sure I'll bear some form of mental scar for the rest of my life now. I've gotten so many that I could start a collection."

Russell wiped his axes clean on *Not-Subulo's* body. "Sorry, boys," he said. "I didn't realize that you were both humongous wussies."

"Hey!" Wesley protested. "Is now really the time to get your sass on?"

Russell grinned. His eyes were filled with the sort of manic fire one might see in a junkie. "I have to get my punches in before I'm responsible for your well being," he said. "Let's go already. The snow will bury this fool, hopefully."

He bent down and retrieved the stone tablet, which, upon closer inspection, was a tombstone, and a fresh one at that, with clods of dirt still clinging to the bottom. The name *Owen* was inscribed upon it, listing a year of birth and death.

"Uh, Russell?" Wesley asked. "Whose tombstone is that?"

"I would've thought it was obvious enough. It's Owen's," Russell said.

"Who exactly is this Owen fellow?"

"Well, Owen is dead, and that's about all I know," Russell said, brushing snow off of the tombstone. "So now I've taken his grave. Don't get too upset, I'll put it back eventually."

Russell laid the tombstone flat on the ground. It was unusually large, at least for tombstone. It could've passed for a memorial of a battle, at least a battle that was light in casualties.

"Hop on," Russell said.

"What, the tombstone?" Jack asked.

"What else?"

Jack and Wesley hesitantly stepped onto the tombstone. It comfortably fit the both of them, leaving just enough room for Russell to squeeze into the front.

"What purpose does this accomplish?" Wesley asked. "We're on a tombstone."

"Well, we're about to partake in my favorite pastime," Russell said.

"Please don't tell me you're planning to rip our heads open," Jack said.

"My second favorite pastime," Russell amended. "Tombstone surfing."

"That sounds omino...*WHOA!*"

The tombstone had begun to float, wobbling for a few seconds before it shot forward. The boys probably would've fallen off, but their feet seemed to have been magically super-glued to the tombstone. They settled for silently praying to any deity that happened to cross their minds for forgiveness, occasionally whimpering as they fought the urge to wet themselves.

The tombstone continued to get faster as they sped towards one of the walls which surrounded the academy.

"We're ramming into the wall, aren't we?" Wesley asked. "You know, if we are, I'm fine with it. I just want to know."

Russell confusedly glanced back. "Why would I do that? We're taking the exit out."

"Well, screw me for trying, I guess," Wesley muttered.

The tombstone veered to the left, where a steady stream of various luxury cars were pouring out of the exit gate. In one swift move, the tombstone leapt into the air, landing on the roof of a silver-white Lexus with a *CRUNCH*. Russell hooted like an insane man as the tombstone proceeded to noisily slide its way down the windshield, dropping onto the road in front of the Lexus.

The cars around them began to honk, indignant drivers peeking out of their windows as Russell sped away from the road.

"Why would you do that?" Jack asked.

"For fun," Russell said. "I usually manage Subulo's paperwork, so this is like heaven for me."

"Subulo has paperwork?" Jack inquired. "What for?"

"Oh, this and that," Russell breezily replied. "Company reports, taxes, the usual stuff."

"That sounds horrendously boring," Wesley said.

"You wouldn't believe it," Russell said. "If I didn't get to murder so many people, I probably would've gone insane from doing all of that stuff."

They swerved into the forest where they'd arrived, greeted by the familiar smell of burnt rubber and smoke. As they cleared the line of trees, they found Subulo in the middle of a chess game with Ruby.

"Hello, boys," he said, not looking up from his game. "Nice of you to join us. Checkmate, Ruby."

"That's not checkmate," Ruby said. "Subulo, you're the black side. You can't move my pieces..."

"Anyway," Subulo said, standing and brushing off his pants, "I'll remove your disguises. I was debating letting you two remain as overweight elderly men forever, but Ruby over here changed my mind, so make sure to give her your highest praise."

Ruby looked mildly amused, turning to Jack and Wesley. "He sucks at games," she whispered, jabbing her thumb towards Subulo.

"I can believe that," Jack said.

"I most definitely do not," Subulo harrumphed, letting out a haughty sniff.

"I beat him three times at *Go Fish* before he agreed to change you back," Ruby continued.

"And I'm regretting my decision," Subulo said, pointing at Jack and Wesley and snapping his fingers. There was an audible *POOF* as Jack felt himself sliding back into the comfortable normality of his own body.

"Many thanks, Ruby," Wesley said. "Those pants were killing me. Subulo, I appreciate the…immersion I felt in the disguise, but why'd you think it was a smart idea to make us both fat and old?"

"As it happens, I can only disguise you as overweight elderly men. I've spent years honing that one transformation to the point of utter mastery. The universe trembled before my power on the day that I perfected it."

"Really?" Wesley asked, an eyebrow raised.

"No," Subulo said. "I just thought it'd be funny. Come help me fish the minivan out of the lake."

## CHAPTER 9

# Subulo Plays His Own Version of "Stop Hitting Yourself"

Croweley sighed with resignation as he felt himself being killed again. The voices in his head wouldn't stop running their mouths. He'd long learned to tune them out, consigning them to the role of mere background noise, only listening when he was immensely bored or seeking advice. Most of the time, they argued. Ferociously. It was like a family gathering when someone brought up politics. It was always about the most mundane of subjects, as well; they would continue an argument about what to have for breakfast long after Croweley had finished eating it.

Croweley's vision abruptly cut off as a large pair of axes turned his eyeballs into mangled, bloody piles of gelatinous flesh. In the ensuing darkness, the voices began to chatter amongst themselves.

*Did you die again, Croweley?*

*Oh, he died? Big surprise.*

*He's so irresponsible. I say that we take charge and rule the body as our own.*

*That's not how it works, you nitwit. He's miles more competent than you could ever hope to be.*

*Curb your tongue! It's not like we've tried, have we?*

"Hey, can you all shut up?" Croweley asked.

*Shut your trap, Croweley,* the voices in his head said in unison, before continuing to argue.

"Well, I tried," he murmured, glancing upwards. "Let's get on with this."

He began to concentrate as the voices continued to shout at each other, imagining his eyes coming back together. A fuzzy image of the world began to piece itself back together, clouded over with a mire of fog and specks of light. He blinked as his eyes reopened, coughing up blood as he took his first breath. His vocal chords had been haphazardly cut into chunks, and every time he breathed a faint whistling noise could be heard coming from the ruined wreck that was his throat. His mouth tasted of vomit and blood.

He attempted to speak, but only managed to make a pitiful vibrating noise with his mouth.

*This'll have to do,* he thought to himself.

He rifled around in the snow for another few seconds before he retrieved his suitcase and cane.

Croweley set off at a sprint, testing how far he could push his body. There appeared to have been a jam at the gate; something about a wrecked Lexus. He cursed. It would be virtually impossible to avoid detection, especially since he was essentially a zombie covered from head to toe in fresh blood. He glanced around before settling on one of the brick walls which surrounded the academy. He pointed at it with the cane. The bricks gleamed with an almost imperceptible sheen as a portal opened. Without pausing, Croweley sprinted directly through it.

The portal dumped him in the lake, soaking his clothes with freezing water. Croweley hurriedly paddled to shore. The mystical regenerative powers that he'd been bestowed with were busying themselves on his eyebrows, piecing them back together one hair at a time.

Croweley moaned in exasperation before he took refuge behind a nearby tree.

It was then that he noticed a strikingly colored minivan half submerged in the lake. It seemed oddly familiar to him, but he couldn't quite figure out why.

Someone was standing at the edge of the lake near Croweley, their long white hair nearly touching the surface of the dark water.

*Wait a second.*

*Whoa, that's Subulo, isn't it? Hold up. Croweley, I think it's high time that you set us free, don't you think? Chop chop.*

*For once, I think we're in agreement. You should definitely get to it right now. Go on. Kill him.*

Croweley's heart began to race. Slowly, he pointed a finger at Subulo.

"I can see you, dipwad," Subulo said, turning to face him.

Oh, *great.*

Subulo snapped his fingers. Croweley attempted to retaliate, but his head exploded.

*Well, that was short-lived. To be frank, I was expecting a bit more than that.*

Croweley gritted his teeth and snapped his fingers. The essential parts of his head- the brain, eyes, and mouth- all flew back towards the approximate location of his head as the rest of the flesh fell into the snow. He stood back up, attempting to convey anger with the limited resources that he had at his disposal. Before Subulo could make Croweley's head explode again, Croweley pointed at him. Great hunks of flesh began to tear themselves off of Subulo, who simply laughed.

"Are you even trying?" he taunted. "Did you think you could kill me with moves like that?"

Subulo pulled out a gun from his belt and aimed it at Croweley. It was oddly shaped, shining black in the light of the winter moon.

"Bang," Subulo said. The barrel elongated into a spike, pursuing Croweley at an unreasonably fast pace. Croweley turned around, grabbing the spike with his hands, but it jabbed its way through his hand. He let go of the gun, grabbing onto one of the ends and breaking it with a CRUNCH. The gun vanished. Croweley whirled to face Subulo, but he was nowhere to be seen.

"Coward," he called. "Come and face me."

"That wasn't the smartest thing to say," Subulo said, reappearing out of thin air. He was holding the strange gun in his hand, which he aimed at Croweley.

Croweley ducked to the side and pointed at Subulo. The hand holding the gun fell off, cut cleanly at the wrist. Subulo regarded it with surprise before looking at Croweley.

"I haven't seen that trick before," he said.

Croweley pointed his finger upwards, and Subulo collapsed, his neck cleanly broken.

"Now you've got my attention," he said. He rose to his feet, bones crunching as he reset his neck. He picked up his hand and reattached it before aiming the gun at Croweley again.

Croweley pointed an identical copy of the gun back at Subulo.

"You've got a lot of tricks, don't you?" he asked. He whistled, and Croweley's gun turned into a crow, which pecked Croweley's hand before taking flight. "Figures. I created you, didn't I?"

Croweley slashed his hand across the air and cut Subulo in half. His two halves trembled in the air for a moment before they forced themselves back together. "I really wish that you hadn't," he dispassionately said. "Every accursed day that I have to spend hunting you down is a day where I could be blissfully enjoying oblivion."

"It wasn't my choice, Croweley. If I had my way, you wouldn't exist," Subulo said. "Obviously, you getting in my way all the time isn't in my best interest. But getting myself killed isn't exactly in my best interests, either."

"Let's move onto more important matters," Croweley said. "Such as why it's in the world's best interests. Letting you roam around is a horrifically bad idea for everyone except for you."

"Regardless, killing me won't solve your problems,"

Subulo said. "You are far too independently developed to be tied to me in any meaningful way anymore."

"You're lying," Croweley said, slashing his hand through the air.

Subulo made an exasperated noise as he was sliced in half again. "This is getting old," he said. "Don't you know that you can't kill me like this? Frankly, I'm embarrassed. I don't mind a good assassination attempt, but at least put in the effort."

Croweley snapped his fingers. Subulo was chopped into fourths, and then eighths, and then sixteenths. As Subulo reassembled himself, Croweley felt his legs abruptly give way from under him. Subulo had his hand out, his expression weary.

"You could've just let me go back and I would've called it even," Subulo said. "I'm insulted to be associated with you. See you later."

He made a fist, and Croweley's head began to swell, threatening to burst. Croweley did the sensible thing and threw his suitcase at Subulo. It nailed him in the head, breaking his concentration. He looked down.

"I'm guessing that's a last resort," he said, looking back up. "Anyway, where was I?"

Croweley made a gesture with his hand reminiscent of the motion one made when opening a door. The suitcase unlatched itself, black slime beginning to ooze out of it. Subulo lurched free of the offending muck, a look of mild disgust upon his face.

"Well, it's not what I'd call a surprise attack, but it certainly was a surprise," he said. "Are we done yet?"

The suitcase's lid was blown off of its hinges as a host of black, writhing limbs appeared from its depths. Subulo's body was jerked around like he was a toy being fought over by a group of rowdy children, being torn apart in the process. Soon, he'd been shred into ribbons of flesh, which gently fluttered to the ground while the limbs withdrew back into the suitcase, the lid securing itself behind them.

The forest was silent for a moment. Croweley hesitantly poked at one of the ribbons with his foot.

"I'd like to restate my previous point," Subulo's voice said. "That wasn't so much of a surprise attack as it was a surprise, Croweley."

His body reassembled itself with remarkable speed, down to the very last piece of fabric on his dress suit.

"See, I don't think you're picking up what I'm throwing down," Subulo said, brushing dust off of his suit. "Killing me doesn't work. It's a no-no. There's no special clause or weird side effect. It's not like yours, either, which is like the diet soda equivalent of immortality. This is the real deal. Both of our times could be more productively spent doing other things. I have a trip to manage, you have a therapist to book. Life goes on. How about it?"

Croweley thought for a moment. "That's gonna be a no from me," he said, holding his hand up. "I'll just assume that you're lying, and that I'll kill you if I try hard enough."

"You're surprisingly stubborn," Subulo said. "But as for

me, I have better things to do. Goodbye. For real, this time."

Croweley felt the ground under him spiral into oblivion as Subulo cheerfully waved. He desperately clawed at the rapidly disappearing ground, but he was soon swallowed by darkness.

He landed on something soft. He could discern that he was in a room; there appeared to be walls and a door. Croweley felt along the walls before discovering that there was a light switch. He flicked it. Nothing happened. Upon closer inspection, Croweley realized that all of the walls were coated in light switches, from the floor to the ceiling.

*Look what you've gotten yourself into, Croweley. Real smart of you.*

"What did you want me to do, if you're so smart?" Croweley demanded, flicking light switches at random. "First, you tell me to kill Subulo and then you tell me I'm dumb for trying to kill Subulo?'

*Well, we weren't the ones who failed, were we?*

"Yeah, so you sit on the sidelines and insult everything that I attempt," Croweley said.

*You're surprisingly bitter.*

*You know, I just now discovered how much I disliked you, Croweley.*

"Ah, good. So the feeling is mutual," Croweley said, continuing to search for the light switch. After several rounds of searching the entire room, Croweley ascertained that all of the light switches were duds, and that Subulo was a humongous jerk, if that hadn't been made clear enough to him already.

He plopped down onto the floor, exhausted. The voices

had stopped talking to him at some point; they were all treating him like he was a dog who'd pissed on a ridiculously expensive carpet.

With nothing particularly better to do, Croweley had explored the room once more. He'd attempted to open the door, only to discover that it was a painted portion of wall. As he attempted to turn the handle, the lights abruptly came on, temporarily blinding him. In the new light, he noticed that a mirror had been leaned against the wall, with a sticky note attached to it. He walked over to it and read the note.

*If you use your imagination, you can pretend that you're both fighting me and that we're equally matched. Have fun. -S*

Croweley felt a wave of impotent rage crash over him. He wanted to punch the mirror, but he was afraid of getting glass buried in his knuckles.

He settled for punching the wall, which, in the new light, turned out to be cushioned. He attempted to slice the walls open, but found that his powers had been nullified.

"Well, great," Croweley said. "What am I supposed to do now?"

*You could think about how badly you messed up.*

*I agree. It would be a wise use of time indeed.*

"That wasn't an invitation for you to speak...nevermind," Croweley said.

"Knock knock," a voice said. Subulo walked into the room directly through the fake door, dressed in a lab coat.

Croweley picked up the mirror and chucked it at him. It passed right through Subulo, bouncing off of the corner and nearly hitting Croweley on its way back.

"That wasn't very nice," Subulo said. "I'm just trying to help, you know."

"What is this place?" Croweley demanded.

Subulo pulled out a clipboard and wrote something on it. "It's your own private hell," he said. "You could call it a pocket dimension. Or the inside of a particularly sadistic TARDIS, if you're a nerd."

"What exactly am I supposed to do in here?"

"Well, ideally you're supposed to die, but you seem to be rather immune to that," Subulo said. "So I've gone ahead and highlighted a treatment plan for your affliction."

He showed Croweley his clipboard, which showed a stick figure labeled *Me* in a lab coat disemboweling another stick figure labeled *You*. Red pen had been used for the resulting gore. An infinity symbol was drawn at the bottom of the page.

Croweley snorted. "You're going to turn my innards into strawberry jam for all eternity? Surely the almighty Subulo has better things to do."

"Oh, I'm not the Subulo," he snorted. "The original sent me here. We go by the same name for the sake of simplicity. Worry not, though. It'll be just as though the real one was here with you."

He pulled out a steel mallet, a large knife, and what looked like a spork, arranging them nearby before he began putting on surgical gloves.

"Uh," Croweley said. "Can I use the restroom before you kill me?"

"'Fraid not," Subulo breezily said. "Don't worry too much, I hear you void your bowels upon death."

"Well, that's something to look forward to," Croweley muttered. "So how does this whole *original* thing even work? Is he your king, and are you his subjects, or is it more of a communist government thing?"

"Why bother with a government when you're all equal?" Subulo asked curiously. "It just makes things more messy. It's like a building full of co-workers, with a manager at the top."

"Does that make you mad?" Croweley asked. "That he gets to rule while you do the menial jobs for him?"

Subulo pondered Croweley's question, although he seemed more intent on deciding what tool to disembowel him with. "No, not really," he said. "Anyway, let's get this started."

## CHAPTER 10

# Jack Struggles to Find His Way Out of a Leather Suitcase

The boys didn't want to help Subulo fish the minivan out of the lake.

"No way am I going back in there," Jack said. "That hunk of scrap on wheels is a lost cause, at this point. It's not worth the hypothermia that I'm going to contract."

Wesley nodded. "Jack's made a good point, for once. The water's too cold."

"Yeah...wait, for once?"

"Well, suit yourself," Subulo said, shrugging his shoulders. "It's not like there's much else to do out here, unless you want to get destroyed at chess by Ruby."

He turned around and walked back into the forest, disappearing from view.

Jack surveyed the clearing. Ruby had leaned back against a tree, wiping dried blood off of her gun with a fluffy yellow dish towel. The chess set lay on the ground next to a pile of cards, rapidly being swallowed by the snow.

"Where did he even get a chess set?" Jack asked Wesley.

"He probably just travels everywhere with several board games stuffed into his suit," Wesley said.

There was a rustling of leaves nearby, and Russell emerged from the forest holding a large dead animal which sort of resembled a boar, in the same way that a packet of instant noodles sort of resembled a healthy and well-balanced meal.

"Russell, *what is that?*" Jack asked.

"Dinner," Russell simply said.

Wesley gagged. "That thing might actually be uglier than the hell-hound. Actually, no. But it is a pretty close third."

"What's second?" Jack asked.

"Subulo," Wesley said.

The animal looked as though it had been conceived on a day where Mother Nature had been drinking, drinking progressively larger amounts and getting more and more drunk as she continued down the body. The animal had all of the trappings of a normal boar; scraggly brown fur, two pairs of hooved legs, and a snout. However, its mouth bristled with sharp, shark-like teeth; along with that, it was covered with glassy, unblinking eyes, which seemed to shift in an uncomfortably lifelike way as Russell plopped the animal down onto the snowy ground.

"Where'd you find an animal like that?" Wesley asked.

"In the forest," Russell said.

"What is this thing called?"

"It's called an all-seeing boar. It likes cold, dark winter forests where it can eat unsuspecting humans without fear of being spotted."

"Well, that's informative," Wesley said. "How are we going to eat it?"

"With your mouths," Russell said, ripping off one of the legs and holding it out to Jack. "We can't build a fire, so we'll have to make do."

"Russell, how many times have I told you to stop feeding my guests raw meat?"

Subulo stepped into the clearing, brushing snow off of his shoulders. "Seriously. At least microwave it or something."

Russell scowled. "I still don't trust those things. Microwaves, or whatever they're called. I'd much rather take a roaring bonfire."

"Unfortunately for you, those are what we call a 'fire hazard'," Subulo said. "Anyways, the minivan's back there."

"Is it functional?" Jack skeptically asked.

Subulo made a noncommittal gesture with his hand. "I got it out of the lake. I have yet to attempt to start it, though."

"I mean, that's already nothing short of a miracle," Jack said. "How'd you manage it?"

"I sacrificed a virgin under the light of the winter moon," Subulo said, striding back into the forest. "Come on. Time's a-wasting."

The van was resting on the shore near the lake as the group broke through the line of trees, bathed in a serene silver light.

"Wow," Wesley said. "I'm...speechless."

"Subulo, we're definitely going to get pulled over if we drive in that," Jack said.

Ruby finished wiping off her gun before sticking her

dishrag back into her pocket. "I've seen worse," she simply said. "But yeah, we probably are."

Subulo sighed. "I did the best I could, alright? We're on a schedule here."

The van had taken a souvenir from its time in the lake; the vehicle was caked with dried, frozen mud. A thick, azure syrup was slowly dripping its way downwards, staining the surrounding snow a shade of light blue.

"Ok, even ignoring the mud, what is that blue stuff?" Wesley asked.

"Antifreeze," Subulo said.

Jack blinked. "Sorry, could you repeat yourself? I could almost have sworn that you said the word *Antifreeze*."

Subulo had a look of confusion upon his face. "Is this not what antifreeze is used for? It seemed pretty self explanatory to me. You pour it over something, and it stops it from freezing."

"That's not...you know what? I don't think now's the time to be having this conversation," Jack said. "Let's just get in the car."

Jack attempted to open the door, only to find his progress hindered by several layers of mud. The handle made a crunching noise before it broke off in Jack's hand.

"Actually, I don't think that's gonna work," he muttered. "Right. Subulo, I'm assuming you don't happen to have a spare car lying around?"

"I have a gently used magic carpet," Subulo suggested. "*Gently used* as in *ripped to shreds by an angry Bengal tiger*."

"Why are you like this?" Wesley asked, burying his face in his hands.

"Look," Subulo said. "I really can't resist a good deal, even it means I'm getting a hunk of junk. Actually, I can't resist discounts in general. Love 'em. Can't get enough. Probably caused by centuries of being ripped off, and then subsequent centuries of living in abject poverty."

"Subulo, we don't have time to deal with your deep-set psychological issues right now," Ruby said. "Do we have an escape ride?"

"Wait a second," Jack said. "Couldn't you, I don't know, open a portal?"

Subulo shrugged. "Well, I could, but portals kind of suck. They always come with caveats. I can only bring others through portals when moving at high speeds, for example."

"What kind of weirdly specific condition is that?" Wesley asked.

"I don't know. I'm still not even sure if that's the specific situation. Portals don't exactly come with user's manuals, you know."

"Focus, people," Ruby said. "We need to get a game plan together."

"Right," Subulo grinned. "What I'm thinking is that we strap Wesley, Jack, and Ruby to the roof while Russell and I push the car."

His proposal was met with a resounding silence.

"Sheesh," he said. "Fine. Party poopers. Let's see if I have anything that I've forgotten about. Hold on a second, I do."

Subulo pulled out a phone from his pocket and punched in a number.

"Hello?" he asked. "Yeah, it's me, Subulo." He paused. "How many other Subulos do you know? Yes, it's me." Another pause. "I need a car. Yeah. One of those will do nicely. Ok, bye." He hung up.

"What was that all about?" Jack asked.

"I've ordered another car," Subulo said, checking his watch. "It should be here any moment."

"What was stopping you from doing that before?"

"Their no-refunds policy," Subulo said. "Never mind that, I think it's coming."

The ground began to rumble below the group as the air grew uncomfortably warm. The wind picked up, shaking leaves loose from trees and ruining Jack's hairdo as it wailed and screeched. Chunks of earth began to loosen as great gouts of hellfire spurted into the air all around them.

"You know, I'm starting to think that the magic carpet you mentioned isn't sounding so bad, after all," Jack said.

The hellfire abruptly dissipated as the ground grew cold once more, the winter air setting in.

"Thanks for buying from Abyssal Automobiles," a woman's voice spoke in the forced cheerfulness mostly associated with live-action commercials for laundry detergent. "The best damned auto company this side of the netherworld."

Silence returned to the group as they looked around.

Jack scratched his head. "Ok, where's the car?"

Jack nearly had his lifespan forcefully shortened as a red minivan fell from the sky, landing on the grass next to him with a soft *THUMP*.

"Are you kidding me?" Wesley asked.

"They have these in bulk order, you know," Subulo said, fondly stroking the front of the vehicle. "Excellent shipping, too."

"We need to find a way to curb your strange fondness of red minivans, Subulo," Jack said. "I'm pretty sure that there are rehab programs for this. At the very least, we could feature you on a TV show."

"Look, the day that these stop becoming the most convenient purchase for me is the day that I give them up," Subulo said. "You laugh now, but you'll be driving one of these suckers soon enough."

"I doubt it," Jack said. "You'll have to force my cold, dead hands onto the steering wheel."

"Let's just get in the minivan," Wesley sighed.

The group filed into the minivan. It had that unidentifiable *new car* smell, an intoxicating combination of warm leather and harmful chemicals.

Subulo started the ignition. The car reeled forward with a sudden burst of speed. "I think this is a good speed," he said to himself. "Alright, folks. If we total a tree, I'd like to say that it's been a tolerable time with you all."

"I wish I could say the same," Wesley said. "Oh, wait. I can't. Because you essentially kidnapped us."

"I do yearn for you to stop bringing that subject up," Subulo said.

As Jack shifted his weight, his foot happened to brush against an object that had been wedged under the seat. He glanced down to discover that it was a slightly battered brown leather suitcase.

"Hey, Subulo," he asked. "Do all of your cars come with complimentary suitcases?"

Subulo's eyes widened as he glanced back. "Chuck that out of the window."

Jack rolled down the window and grabbed the suitcase, but it held fast, attaching itself to his hand. No matter how hard he shook it, it was stuck to his palm.

"It's not letting go," Jack said. "This is probably a cause for alarm."

"How'd you reach that conclusion?" Subulo muttered. "Jack, I'm going to cut off your hand. Keep it outside of the window while I roll it up."

Jack felt sweat begin to bead on his brow as his palms moistened. "Uhhh," he said. "Are you sure? I quite like my hand."

"Subulo, that's messed up," Wesley said. "You probably shouldn't do that."

"I don't have time for this," Subulo muttered. "Jack, that suitcase is far more important than any given number of your limbs. If it's stuck, then I'm going to have to cut your hand off."

Jack opened his mouth in protest, but was cut off as the suitcase's latches loosened. A black wave of sludge oozed out of the cracks, coating his hand in a thick, sticky slime. Soon,

Jack could no longer feel his hand. He began to frantically shake as the slime continued to creep up his arm.

Subulo pursed his lips and began to roll up the window. Jack clenched his teeth and concentrated on not passing out from fear.

The black sludge had nearly reached his elbow when the suitcase fully opened.

The van's windows abruptly shattered as the minivan spun out of control, nearly smashing into a thick wall of evergreens. The slime suddenly vanished back into the open suitcase, which had begun to glow a brilliant shade of white.

Jack felt panic begin to overtake him as he saw his arm vanishing into the suitcase.

"Russell, cut off Jack's arm," Subulo barked. "Do it quickly."

Russell heaved a sigh and looked at Jack. "Sorry about this, boy," he said, pulling out an ax from his belt.

Jack looked on in astonished horror as the axe bounced off of his arm, which had seemingly become as solid as steel. The suitcase had already consumed most of his arm.

"Forget this," Subulo said. "Wesley, push Jack out of the car."

"I'm not doing that," Wesley said, crossing his arms.

"Why must I do everything myself?" Subulo asked. He snapped his fingers, and Jack felt himself being flung out of the vehicle.

He barely had time to scream before the suitcase swallowed him whole.

Jack was in a padded cell. For some odd reason, it was covered in light switches. Two bloody corpses were huddled in the corner, streaks of vital fluid smearing the walls. He suppressed the urge to vomit as the smell hit him; the heady scent of fresh blood, mixed with a healthy dose of rot and decay. A broken mirror lay on its side nearby, shards of glass lining the floor.

"Oh, so you're here."

Jack's heart leapt into his throat as one of the corpses in the corner raised its head, an expression of mild boredom on its face. "I was wondering who I'd grabbed."

"You're Subulo," he said.

"No, I'm not," the corpse said. "Common misconception. I'm Croweley."

"Well, Croweley," Jack said. "It's been nice and all, but I have business elsewhere. So, I'm just going to leave."

"You can't, at least not without my permission," Croweley said. "You can try, I won't stop you."

Jack turned around and attempted to walk through the door, only to find that it was a fake, painted onto the padded wall.

"Well, great," he said.

"That's right," Croweley rasped. "You can't leave."

"I can see that," Jack said. "Who's that, um, fellow next to you?"

"He's my torturer," Croweley said. "Or he was my torturer. I killed him, of course."

Jack nervously eyed the corpse. "Great," he said. "So, Croweley, why'd Subulo want to torture you exactly?"

Croweley shrugged. "For existing, I suppose. I'm essentially just a bag of flesh where he stored his negative feelings. I was just a talisman, in the beginning. Something to help ease his pain. After his inevitable loss of faith in all he held dear, I grew quite a lot. He's got a lot of demons that he's locked up inside of me, and now he wants them to disappear. He's discovered that he can't completely kill me, so he's done the second best thing."

"That's wonderful, Croweley, but what exactly am I doing in here?"

Croweley brightened up. "I'm so glad you asked!" he said. "I brought you in here using the suitcase. I can do that, can you believe it?"

"This is the inside of a suitcase?" Jack asked.

"Awfully inquisitive, aren't you? No, this isn't the suitcase. To quote a certain someone..." He nudged the corpse next to him. "This is a pocket dimension, of sorts. I just brought you here using the suitcase."

"You know, I hate to ask this, but why'd you bring me here?" Jack hesitantly asked.

Croweley grinned. "Why, I thought that was obvious. I brought you here to kill you."

## CHAPTER 11

# Subulo Files Some Paperwork

"Sorry, but what just happened?" Ruby asked.

Wesley was peering out of the van's window as they sped away. "Well, Ruby, it would appear as though my best friend's been eaten by a suitcase."

"Take heart, Wesley, he was screwed the moment he touched that suitcase," Subulo said. "There was literally nothing we could've done to save him."

"You know, Subulo, I don't find that very comforting for some reason," Wesley said. "Thanks for trying, though."

"Always happy to serve," Subulo said. "We should have just enough time to escape while your friend is trapped inside the suitcase."

"He is still alive, right?" Wesley asked.

Subulo shrugged from the front. "I'd spare your feelings and tell you that he was, but I frankly have no idea."

The van hit a particularly large tree, plunging the group into darkness.

"Ok, the suitcase shouldn't be able to reach us from here," Subulo said. The van emerged from the portal and promptly plowed through a gravestone, scattering dirt and snow as it backed up. They'd appeared in a thickly wooded cemetery. Snow was falling from the sky, obscuring the graveyard dirt. The tips of tombstones were visible poking out above the snow, almost buried beneath the mounds of white. The air was unbearably cold, making the whole group collectively shiver as one. The night sky was clear and dark, and the stars shone with an infinite, radiant beauty. Wesley had never seen stars like these before. Bright and refined, they made all the stars that he'd previously admired seem ugly and imperfect.

"Where are we?" Wesley asked, glancing around him.

"Iceland," Subulo said. "This lovely little cemetery is called…you know what? I'm not even going to attempt to pronounce the name."

"Hólavallagarður," Russell murmured, bending down to examine one of the tombstones.

"Gesundheit," Ruby said.

"No, Hólavallagarður's the name of this place. It means *garden on a hill.*"

"Are all Icelandic names this hard to pronounce?" Wesley asked.

"You wouldn't believe it," Russell said, wiping snow off of the tombstone he was examining. "There was this famous volcano that everyone was talking about, and nobody pronounced it right. Thankfully, Icelandic people undergo rigorous training to pronounce their words correctly. Those who can't make the proper spitting noise when saying *Vaðlaheiðarvegavinnuverkfærageymsluskúraútidyralyklakippuhringur* are socially ostracized for the rest of their lives."

"Really?" Ruby asked.

"Sadly, no," Russell said.

Subulo walked over to the group carrying three large shovels. "Alright, folks, let's get this show on the road," he said.

"Are we robbing graves?" Wesley asked, an expression of horror on his face.

"Quite the opposite, actually," Subulo said. "We're digging Russell a spot where we can lay him to rest."

"Why would we do that, exactly?" Ruby asked. "Are we burying him alive?"

Subulo frowned. "Did you forget to tell them about your, ah, condition, Russell?"

Russell bemusedly scratched his head. "Well, the thing is," he sheepishly said. "I'm dead. Well, no, that's not right. I'm undead, I suppose you would say."

"You're a zombie?" Ruby curiously asked. "You don't look the part."

"Well, I had the gall to attempt to live in Iceland," Russell said, a bitter expression crossing his face. "I starved to death in the winter after my crops died. I usually got by, by plundering villages with my clansmen, but I was sentenced to exile after I murdered several people in a drunken brawl. Subulo found me kicking about in Hell and smuggled me back in his car."

"Those were the days," Subulo dreamily said. "The world was young and fresh, and you could bring a buddy back from death in the course of a single afternoon."

"What happened?" Wesley asked curiously.

"Too many politicians wound up down there," Subulo morosely pronounced. "They began to demand rights for the damned before the lord of Hell- Satan, you would call him- finally had enough and sent a message by encircling Hell's limits with great stone boundaries, so that the damned could no longer escape."

"Anyways," Russell said. "I can only be on the surface for limited amounts of time. I have to be kept cold, or I start to rot."

"Ew," Wesley said.

"Precisely."

"But wouldn't having a zombie super-warrior by our side help us, even if he's slightly decayed?" Ruby protested.

"Well, I'm taking you both back to the office to fill out paperwork, so not really," Subulo said. "Teams to send after the suitcase, forms to dispatch a rescue team to send inside the suitcase, confidential papers pertaining to my assignment that have to be burned, so on and so forth."

"I suppose that makes sense," Ruby said. "Still disappointing, though."

The snow continued to fall as the three of them dug the grave in silence. It was monstrously hard work; the dirt was almost frozen solid. After a good ten minutes of sweating and panting, the group stepped back and admired their handiwork.

"I think that's deep enough," Wesley said.

Subulo inspected the grave and then frowned. "Go a little deeper."

"What?" Ruby asked. "This is more than enough for a single person, Subulo."

"In case you haven't noticed, Ruby, Russell is not exactly the size of the average person."

"Fair point," Ruby said, resuming her digging. After another few minutes, Subulo nodded.

"This should be enough," he said, pulling himself up and out of the grave. "Hold still, Wesley."

Wesley regarded Subulo in confusion. "I am holding still. What's that supposed to mean?"

"Bang," Subulo said, pulling his gun out from his tuxedo.

Wesley barely had time to blink before the spike pierced through his skull. He began to scream and claw at the ever-protruding spike in his forehead, like some sort of bizarre bloody unicorn horn. Ruby finished uttering an expletive and almost managed to jump out of the grave before she was skewered, as well. She fell with a soft *THUMP* back into the grave before she began to bleed.

"I am in immense pain," she breathed, and then promptly died.

"That was quick. Finish the burial, Russell," Subulo said, tucking the gun back into his belt.

Russell nodded. "Sure thing," he said, picking up the shovel and scooping the dirt back into the grave. "We should try giving them an honest fight next time."

"Why would we do that?" Subulo asked. "Not giving them one has worked thus far, hasn't it?"

"It would add some more variety to the proceedings, at

least," Russell said. "Although I admit it's harder to feel empathy for them after all these times."

"I think I stopped caring after the tenth time I had to do this," Subulo said, reaching back into his pocket and pulling out his phone. He punched in a number and waited.

"Hello, this is Subulo," he said. "The job's done. Just wanted to let you know. We'll be moving on now."

Subulo put the phone back in his pocket. "You done yet, Russell?"

"Just about," Russell said, shoveling the last handful of dirt back into the grave. "Alright. Let's go."

"You're driving this time," Subulo said. "I have to fill in the report."

"Sure."

Subulo slid into the passenger seat of the minivan as Russell started the engine.

"We're going back to my house first, right?" Russell asked.

"Yeah," Subulo said. "No need to open a portal. You know the way there?"

"Obviously."

As the car sped away from the cemetery, Subulo reached down below the passenger seat and retrieved a thick, leather bound book. He turned to a bookmarked page and drew out a pen.

"So, what was different this time?" Subulo asked.

"I'm pretty sure Wesley had red hair when we encountered him in the prior world," Russell said.

"That's a good one and Jack wasn't killed by Croweley

in that world as he will be soon in this one. Hmmm, I did manage to kill both Ruby and Wesley after they dug the grave. Jack and Wesley are from Houston. Different time period, of course. Wesley couldn't open portals this time... oh, what a pain that was to kill him that time."

"How many of their conversations did you record?"

"Most of them, if not all," Subulo absentmindedly said, leafing through the book. "Ugh. I need record Jack's cause of death. Can we just say that he was stabbed by Croweley?"

"I think you'll have to stick around to witness it," Russell said. "There's literally infinite amount of ways that Croweley could kill him in there."

"But we left the suitcase," Subulo complained. "That's Croweley's object, not mine."

"I do see your point," Russell said. "We can probably assume that Jack hasn't somehow acquired the ability to escape certain death in this one instance of reality. Just mark him down as deceased."

"You don't need to tell me twice," Subulo said, closing the book. "Alright. Paperwork's done, now I just need to file it."

The van veered onto a dirt road, heading straight for a huge patch of grass. It stopped in front of a small, abandoned log cabin, spraying soil as it screeched to a halt.

Subulo exited the van, tucking the book under his arm before he opened the unlocked front door. He switched on the lights, bathing the cabin in a warm, yellow glow. He plopped the book down on a nearby wooden table, sending up a cloud of dust. An empty stone coffin lay in the center of the living room, which Russell promptly lay in, sighing with pleasure. Subulo walked to the refrigerator, withdrawing a large bag of ice cubes and tossing it to Russell before he walked back to the book. "Are there any more details that you want to add to the report, Russell?"

Russell yawned. "Croweley tried to kill you?"

"Oh, yeah. He seems to be getting more active, don't you think?"

"That's not of our concern," Russell said. "He's not even a match for you, let alone us."

"I suppose you're right. But it's still something to keep an eye out for. Wouldn't want him to give us grief later."

"True," Russell sleepily said, his speech slightly slurred. "I'm just gonna..."

Russell passed out in the coffin.

Subulo sighed and tapped the book, which made a squawking noise before it turned into a bird with leather-patterned wings.

"You know the drill," Subulo said, sighing as he sat in one of the uncomfortable wooden chairs.

"I need a coffee, and possibly several pounds of narcotics," Subulo declared to no one as he began to search through the pantry, disappointed at the lack of mind-altering substances. The coffee machine made burbling noises as he emptied coffee grounds and water into it before walking away.

Subulo leaned against Russell's coffin and drummed his fingers on the floor.

There was a knock at the window. The bird was back.

"That was surprisingly quick," Subulo said, opening the window and tapping the bird. He licked his finger and turned the pages of the newly transformed tome. "Hey, Russell, come check the new assignment out."

"What?" Russell muttered, blearily rising from the coffin. "Is it paperwork or brutal murder?"

"It's probably just the same old," Subulo said. "Same time period, and we can pick the people again. Well, this'll save me some time. Ready to go now, Russell?"

"Can we take the coffin?" Russell asked.

"'Fraid not," Subulo said. "Business is business, you know how it is."

Russell sighed. "Alright, alright," he said. "Let's get in the van."

Subulo hefted the book as the two men walked back out of the cabin, shutting off the lights on the way out.

"I'm driving this time," Subulo said. "Isn't there a cliff nearby?"

"I believe so," Russell said. "I can look on the internet for a map."

"Don't worry. I think the cabin should be fine, actually."

"Try not to destroy it," Russell said.

"Will do," Subulo said, gunning the engine.

The minivan leaped forward and crashed into the cabin, spraying wood splinters everywhere.

"Of course you nail the portal placement every time it's not my house," Russell said.

"You're over-thinking it," Subulo said. "I'm just

horrendously unlucky at aiming when it comes to your humble abode in particular."

Russell quietly face-palmed as Subulo reversed the car. He sped forward once more and crashed into the cabin again.

"I'm pretty sure you just crushed the coffin," Russell said. "Along with several other pieces of my furniture. You know, I'm starting to think you're doing this on purpose."

Subulo snickered. "Ok, fair's fair. I didn't put up a portal that time. Third time's the charm, though."

Wood crunched under the wheels of the van as it reversed once again, plowing through wood chips as it passed through the portal.

The portal spat them out into a land of endless gray space, stretching out for as far as the eye could see. In the distance, a large white building seemed to tower infinitely upwards, stretching up to incomprehensible heights.

"Work sweet work," Subulo muttered. "I get to meet my accursed fellow employees."

He pushed on the pedal, but the van simply careened through the air making vague grinding noises, its wheels unable to gain traction on the empty air.

"Forget this," Subulo said. "Russell, we're ditching the car."

They exited the van as it drifted away, deciding on doggy-paddling the rest of the way to the building. As they approached, Subulo grabbed onto one of the fake potted plants dotted near the entrance before pulling himself onto stable ground. A set of stairs led to a pair of automatic doors. A large, red-skinned ogre with large, bushy eyebrows sat on the steps smoking a pipe. He was wearing a suit just small enough to accentuate his hideously large beer belly. As Subulo approached, he offered up a generous welcoming gift of a hearty belch.

"Morning, Subulo," he rumbled, blowing a cloud of smoke away from Subulo's general direction.

"Morning, ogre," Subulo said.

"I wish you'd remember my name. 'Ogre' tends to grate on the nerves after centuries of people calling you that. Especially when they're usually screaming it through heaping mouthfuls of their own internal organs."

"I wouldn't want to mispronounce your name and offend you," Subulo said. "I'd best be on my way, I have paperwork to file."

"Later," the ogre said, sticking the pipe back in his mouth.

"I hate my co-workers," Subulo muttered as they shuffled into the lobby, a rather large room with leather easy chairs, more fake potted plants, and a television screen blasting assorted footage of happy people *and aliens, and eldritch beings* all doing activities deemed suitably positive, such as playing fetch with the neighbor's dog or going out for a thrilling campaign for total universal domination. The footage had been playing nonstop ever since the company had instated a *positivity department* after their employees started sending hate mail to the company's P.O. box. The lobby was almost completely empty; most of the employees were either at their cubicles or out on assignments.

"Give your coworkers a chance," Russell said. "They're not that bad."

"Russell, I hate them almost as much as I hate myself, and that's saying quite a lot."

"I do wish you'd stop saying that."

They stepped into an elevator which was impossibly large on the inside, stretching out unbroken for miles on each side. The walls and ceiling were positively bristling with buttons corresponding to different floors. Subulo counted floors with an outstretched finger for a few moments before selecting the six hundred and sixty sixth one.

More positivity programs played as the elevator began its ascent. After a couple of seconds, the doors opened, revealing two oaken doors. A bronze plaque labeled *S and R* rested on the door.

Subulo pulled out a key ring from his pocket before he unlocked the door. Light spilled into their office, a respectably-sized room with a wooden desk, two chairs, and a large red doomsday button, which had been haphazardly shoved next to a stack of books and a slightly battered beanie baby.

Russell sat down in one of the chairs and tapped on the keyboard. After a moment of waiting for the computer to boot, he began typing out an email, occasionally glancing at the book for reference. Meanwhile, Subulo had fished out a power chord attached to the button and plugged it into a nearby outlet. The button began to menacingly glow.

"How long till I press the button?" Subulo asked.

Russell didn't look up from the computer. "The world-destroying one, right?"

"How many buttons do we own? Yes, that one."

"You can do it whenever you want," Russell said.

"Alright."

Subulo went silent for a moment.

"What'd you think of the world?" Russell asked.

"The one we just left?"

"Yeah."

Subulo shrugged. "Eh. Pretty boring. Let's hope the next time's better, huh?"

Subulo pushed the button.

## CHAPTER 12

# Jack Redefines the Word "Meaningless"

Jack blinked as Crowley grinned menacingly at him.

"Sorry, I must've misheard you," Jack said. "You're going to do what exactly?"

"I thought I made myself perfectly clear," Crowley said. "I'm going to kill you."

Jack desperately thought of a response, but could find none. Nervous sweat began to bead on his brow.

At long last, he wearily sighed. "Ok, then," he said. "Get it over with."

Crowley's expression turned into one of surprise. "That's it?"

"What were you expecting?" Jackson asked.

"Correct me if I'm wrong, but shouldn't you be attempting to run away from your inevitable demise?" Crowley asked. "Killing someone's no longer fun if they just stand there and take it."

"Frankly, Crowley, although I've only known you for about five minutes, you're already beginning to disgust me," Jack said, hoping that Crowley didn't see his trembling hands. "I'm screwed either way, so if my final act will be to deny you of any fun, I find that I'm surprisingly fine with that."

Croweley contemplated Jack for a few seconds before he pulled out a large knife.

Great.

"Oh, well," Croweley said, a look of slight disappointment upon his face. "I suppose I'll just have to make do."

Jack attempted to kick Croweley in the groin and grunted in pain as he stubbed his toes. Croweley regarded Jack with slight amusement as he plunged the knife into Jack's chest.

Jack felt as though someone was rubbing a large chunk of his torso raw with a red-hot poker, pausing only occasionally to splash boiling acid onto the open wounds. His vision had begun to fade out. He glanced down at what had used to be a perfectly good upper body and found that it had been replaced with what looked like the contents of a butcher shop's dumpster after a long day of work.

"Why aren't you screaming?" Croweley asked, idly wriggling the knife around in Jack's chest cavity. "It's more entertaining, you know."

Jack attempted to make a witty retort, instead making a noise like a burst water balloon as his lungs started to fill with his own blood. He found that it was becoming rather hard to breathe. His vision began to dim, as a chill settled upon him. Croweley's face seemed to be rippling as the padded cell drifted in and out of focus.

Jack dribbled a thick stream of blood from his mouth.

"Ouch," he said.

Jack died.

~

He found that it wasn't all that unpleasant of an experience. He no longer could feel any pain, and instead was surrounded by the kind of all-encompassing peace that one gets from successfully running away from their problems. It was like falling asleep at the end of a particularly long day.

He was comfortably warm, and surrounded by something incredibly soft and luxurious. Jack heard birds chirping nearby and smelled the scent of flowers filling the air.

He took a deep breath and opened his eyes.

He was sprawled in a green meadow. Mellow, buttery sunlight bathed his face in a golden glow.

"Am I in heaven?" he wondered aloud.

Almost as soon as the sentence had left his lips, a burning cigarette butt landed inches away from his face, spraying specks of red-hot ash.

"You're not," a voice nearby said. "Far from it, in fact."

Jack stood up. A man with cherry-red skin stood nearby, a brown cloak hastily slung across his shoulders. He gave Jack an amused smile.

"If this isn't heaven, then where am I?" Jack asked, glancing around him. "Also, what's with your skin?"

"You're in...actually, if I knew where we were, I probably would've ditched this place a long time ago," the man said. His voice was oddly thick and slurred, as though he had a cold. "About the skin, well, it's a long story, preferably one that I can tell you later." He pulled out another cigarette and offered it to Jack. "Want a smoke?"

"No thanks," Jack said.

"Suit yourself. There's not much else you can do here besides kill birds and look at grass," the man said, breathing out a puff of smoke.

"Who are you?" Jack asked.

"I'd tell you, but you wouldn't believe me." The man took another drag on his cigarette and coughed. "Those things are awful," he wheezed, letting the cigarette fall out of his mouth and into the grass.

"Why do you keep smoking them, then?"

"Well, I'd acquired an unlimited supply of them a long time ago from a friend of mine. No one's around to share them with, so I figured I'd take advantage, at least."

He paused for a moment.

"This is quite boring," he said. "Let's go to my house."

Jack looked around him. He was surrounded by an endless field of grass and flowers, stretching unbroken towards the horizon.

"Your house? Do you just lie in the grass and fall asleep?" Jack asked, glancing around.

"No. My house is further along. Although sleeping in the grass is an appealing idea, I happen to be allergic to the stuff," the man said. "That's why my voice sounds so... excuse me." He pulled out a tissue from his pocket and sneezed into it, tossing it over his shoulder as the pair began to walk.

"Isn't that littering?"

"Not really," the man said. "Everything that touches

the ground burns up on contact. There are exceptions, of course. Like you."

"Shouldn't the grass be burning up, then?"

"It isn't flammable. It's also unable to get squashed, dirtied, polluted, or otherwise affected in any noticeable way. It's also edible, for some reason."

"What the..."

"Yeah, I know. It's weird," the man said. "Don't even get me started on the flowers."

"What's with this place?" Jack asked.

"Again, if I knew, I'd probably be anywhere in the universe except for here," the man said. "I was sent here quite some time ago for...for something. I think it was because I was kidnapped."

"Your tone's a bit casual for a kidnapping victim," Jack noted.

"Well, I can't even remember the experience," the man said. "It's been quite a while since I arrived here."

As the two of them strolled the grass, an indistinct brown shape appeared in the distance. It soon became clear that it was a house, a picturesque small cottage with a brick chimney cheerfully puffing out clouds of white smoke. The battered earth that they were walking upon soon turned into gravel. The plants seemed more varied in the dirt around the house; flowers of all shapes, sizes, and hues were generously spread throughout the grass. Although Jack was woefully lacking in botanical knowledge, he could appreciate the multicolored beauty which smiled upon him.

The man walked up behind Jack and made a contemptuous noise in his throat as he gazed at the flowers, spitting into a nearby clump of chrysanthemums.

"What was that for?" Jack asked, bewildered.

"I hate these things," the man snuffled. "I've been living in an eternal state of hay fever thanks to them. I suppose it might be nice to wake up to flowers, but these things produce pollen like you wouldn't believe." He grumpily pulled out another tissue and noisily blew his nose, making a sound like a defunct trumpet. "Let's get inside."

The man opened the cottage's painted wooden door. Jack's nostrils were immediately assaulted with the spicy, aromatic scent of cinnamon. Jack stepped through the threshold of the house. The floor was covered in a knitted woolen carpet, which was somehow even softer than the grass outside. Two wooden rocking chairs sat facing a merrily crackling fireplace in the den. The man took off his cloak and hung it on a nearby coat rack.

"Cinnamon's better than pollen," the man said, slumping into one of the rocking chairs. "Sit with me, Jack. I'm only comfortable next to the fire nowadays."

Jack hesitantly sat in the rocking chair next to the man. The flames in the hearth cast a glow across the man's face, bringing his creases and wrinkles into sharp relief. His face was craggy and decrepit, like a once-majestic cliff laid low by an unrelenting sea. His gaze was unfocused and blank as he stared into the writhing sea of orange, his mind wandering elsewhere.

Just as Jack began to wonder if he'd fallen asleep, the

man suddenly shot upwards from the chair, causing Jack to jump.

"I just remembered something," the man proclaimed.

"What is it?" Jack asked, still startled by the sudden movement.

"My name," the man sheepishly said. "It's Blaze."

"You forgot your...never mind," Jack said. "Blaze, I have some questions for you."

"You do?" Blaze curiously asked. "Well, fire away, I suppose."

"I'm not saying that this place isn't nice, but what exactly am I doing here?" Jack asked. "You've told me that I'm not in heaven, but is this an afterlife of some sort?"

"How presumptuous of you to assume there is an afterlife," Blaze haughtily sniffed. "Humans have the unfortunate habit of making up solutions to their problems, and the concept of an *afterlife* is just one of numerous examples. Humanity possesses a crippling fear of death even as it lives, making up stories of eternal pleasure for the worthy amongst it to ward against the realization that everything that it could possibly accomplish would be but a grain of sand in the expansive beaches of the universe. Humanity can only hope to cling to these stories for consolation as it is plunged headfirst into the cold, unfeeling void."

"There's not an afterlife?"

"No, there is," Blaze said. "There are multiple ones, in fact. And you happen to be in precisely none of them. I've brought you here."

"Why'd you bring me here?" Jack asked.

Blaze sighed. "Well, if you're here, there's really no point in sugarcoating it. You've failed. Horribly."

Jack blinked. "What do you mean?"

"You may not have realized it, but you were Subulo's guinea pig for the entire duration of your little adventure," Blaze said.

"I was Subulo's...oh. I see," Jack murmured thoughtfully. "Yeah, that does make sense. What exactly was he using me for?"

"Subulo happens to work for a very large company," Blaze said. "I'm not talking normal large, either. I'm talking subjugation of all known reality large. They've got so many resources at their disposal that it's almost beyond comprehension. They were behind many of the calamities that have occurred throughout history. The dinosaurs were perhaps the only ones who could've taken them on, but the rebellion was crushed. The only entities left who could possibly pose a threat to them are ones like me, who manifest themselves across several different realities. I suppose you could call us gods, but I do hate to use that word. I don't feel very godlike on the average day, so I'm inclined to believe that I'm just a powerful immortal dude."

"You're kind of losing me here," Jack said. "How can you be in different realities if there's only one 'reality'? Plus, if you're present in multiple realities, how can you even be killed? Wouldn't the Blaze that's only exclusive to the particular reality be killed?"

Blaze rubbed his forehead. "Ok, let me try to explain. So,

reality is kind of like an incredibly complex math problem. You can't possibly even solve the math equation, let alone understand the principles that allow that sort of problem to be formed in the first place. Plus, if you think about it too much, something bad is definitely bound to happen to your brain. My advice is not to think about it at all. All you need to know right now is that I am safe here, and the company hasn't managed to find me yet. The keys to determining my location appear to be you, Wesley, and Ruby."

"We are?" Jack asked.

"Yeah," Blaze said. "That much I know. Although I sometimes question the logic of whoever picked you all."

"Hey!"

"It's alright. Wesley and Ruby are probably dead now, as well. Them, and eventually your entire reality. You can rest assured that it's completely your fault. They were dead the moment you got sucked into the suitcase," Blaze said, a mild smile appearing on his face. "Liberating, isn't it? At least there's no way you can top that."

Jack went pale. "They're dead?"

Blaze nodded. "Without a doubt. If you're gone, Subulo will cut his losses and try another reality, deleting yours in the process."

"How exactly does he..." Jack gulped.

"I'm not terribly familiar with the subject, but I believe every employee has a huge red button on their desk," Blaze said. "I'm pretty sure Subulo drew a smiley face on his."

"How do you know that?" Jack asked. "Speaking of which,

how're you so knowledgeable about how Subulo works? Shouldn't you know essentially nothing if you're stuck here?"

Blaze glanced at a clock hanging above the fireplace. "I think you'll be going soon," he said. "Let me take you somewhere before you leave."

"That literally answered none of my questions," Jack complained, following Blaze out of the house.

They walked back down the gravel path, the ground crunching under their feet. The smell of cinnamon faded from behind them as they left. Flowers became less and less frequent as the grass began to grow in unruly clumps, getting taller and taller the further they went. Trees began to dot the landscape, their spiny, twisted branches devoid of any leaves. The sky above them had turned a bland, eggshell white. The grass gradually gave way to brambles and thorn bushes, their sharp spines pricking Jack as he hurried past them. Blaze, seemingly unfazed, forged ahead, looking around.

All at once, Blaze stopped, causing Jack to rather embarrassingly crash into him before righting himself once more.

"We're here," Blaze said.

They'd arrived at a large patch of barren, scorched earth. An assortment of porcelain urns had been neatly arranged into rows along the dirt. They were wildly varied from one urn to the next; one was enameled and showed patterns of waves, another was covered in elaborate drawings of snarling animals.

"What are these for?" Jack asked.

"These hold the ones who came before you," Blaze said.

"The other Jacks, I'd suppose you'd call them. They've told me all sorts of interesting things about their worlds. I've pieced together my understanding of Subulo and what he does from all of their accounts. And this will be your final resting place, as well."

"Haven't I died already, though?" Jack asked.

"Nope," Blaze said. "That was your first death. The second one is permanent."

"Of course it is," Jack said. "I hope you're not planning to stuff me into an urn."

"As entertaining as that would be, no," Blaze said. "You'll turn into dust soon. It always happens a little while after the button is pressed. As long as you're here, I can shield you a little from the effects, but you'll die all the same. If it helps, you would've died even if I hadn't brought you here."

"What does it feel like?" Jack asked. "Turning into dust, I mean."

"Well, I haven't experienced it myself, but I've heard that it's pretty painless. At the very least, I've never heard exceptionally loud screaming when it happens," Blaze said, "

"Well, that's comforting, I suppose."

"Yeah."

Jack stared out at the porcelain jars. "Did I really accomplish anything? From your perspective, at least. Will I be worth mentioning?"

Blaze thought for a moment. "No, not really," he finally said. "You lead a pretty uneventful life, accomplished essentially nothing, and then got brutally murdered. It's almost ironic that you were exceptionally average, at least among the ones resting here."

"Oh," Jack said, in a rather small voice. "I see."

Blaze looked down at Jackson's shoes. "It's starting," he said. "Well, I guess this is goodbye, Jack."

Jackson glanced downwards. His sneakers had begun to crumble into a fine gray powder, snaking up towards the rest of his body. His feet went numb, then his knees. He collapsed onto the ground as the last of his legs disappeared. As the last remnants of Jackson's flesh flaked away, his life flashed before him in a rather cheesy slide-show, although there were more moments that he deemed cringe-worthy rather than heart-warming.

Jack's last sight was of the rows of porcelain urns looming in front of his fading vision. I hope he picks something dignified to put me in, Jackson thought.

Jackson died. Again.

# Epilogue

The sky was dark and overcast, fat, swollen clouds lurking overhead as though waiting for the perfect moment to ruin Jackson's day.

However, Jackson wasn't the type to be daunted by the prospect of a little rain. He merrily whistled a tune as he strode down a gray concrete sidewalk, his head held proudly up high.

The winter holiday had brought many new opportunities for Jackson to really step up his academic performance. Although he was renowned for being an overachiever, he felt that the upcoming finals would be the perfect way to really distinguish himself. He'd done the study guides the day they'd been handed out, and had devoted himself to learning as much as he could.

Jackson stopped on the road to adjust his favorite overlarge Christmas sweater, which had slipped a little on his shoulders. It was Jackson's favorite sweater; it was warm, snug, and had Santa's face on the front, which checked off all three of Jackson's criterion for a perfect Christmas sweater.

Jackson arrived at his bus stop, which consisted of a

humble wooden bench situated at the corner of the sidewalk. Although it was perched atop a sewer, Jackson thought it was a worthy trade-off if it meant that he could enjoy some peace and quiet once in a while.

Jackson sat on the bench and smiled as someone else sat down next to him. He was always up for a little social interaction.

"Hello..."

Jackson blinked in surprise. There was nobody sitting next to him on the bench, after all. He had the strangest feeling of déjà vu, but he shook it off. As he glanced down, he realized that there was something next to him on the bench; a rather battered brown leather suitcase. Jackson wondered if it belonged to someone, and whether he should try to return it to them.

Before he could make up his mind, a raindrop hit the top of his head. Jackson glanced up to see that it was raining. Jackson pulled out an umbrella that he'd stuck in his pocket, opening it with a *CLICK*. He pulled off his sweater and draped it over the suitcase, hoping that it would be enough to prevent it from getting soaked. Hoisting his umbrella above him, Jackson hurried home.

As his feet pounded on the pavement, Jackson had the strangest urge to look behind him. He snuck the barest glance behind him back at the old wooden bench before his eyes widened in surprise.

Both the sweater and the suitcase had vanished.

# About the Author

Alex, also known as "Chippy" by a few particularly aggravating pests in his life, is a high schooler who wishes on almost a daily basis that his life was more interesting. His hobbies include fantasizing about situations which will almost definitely not happen, annoying his friends, and spinning around in swivel chairs.

Alex aspires to one day not commit a faux pas every time he attends a party, and he is currently the subject of a top secret government experiment to turn crippling social anxiety into a form of renewable energy, which has witnessed unprecedented success since his arrival.

# Thanks to:

My schools, Stratford, SBAI, and Spring Forest, for preparing me for the future and scarring me for life in the process.

My friends, who provided me with plenty of insults that my characters could use on each other.

My family, who were with me through this difficult journey (nagging me every step of the way, but still).

My editor, who never lost faith in me even when I was dumb.

My publisher, who shared my editor's faith and also agreed to publish this steaming garbage heap of a book.

My 8th grade English teacher, who made me write a lot. The wonderful people down at the iWRITE Youth Club, who took the time out of their day to provide feedback for me.

The universe at large, which abused me enough that I started to laugh about it.

My readers, who not only read this book, but also bought it for actual money (holy cow).